Praise for
Kristine Kathryn Rusch

"A dark, yet fascinating tale, *The Enemy Within* gives readers an intriguing look at what could have happened in 1964 New York."
—*RT Book Reviews* on *The Enemy Within*

"Deeply evocative, it breathes menace from every page and memorably conveys what Rusch calls the 'casual evil' that suffused Germany as the Nazis came to power."
—The *Daily Mail* (London)
on *Hitler's Angel*

"Told in roughly alternating chapters set in 1913 and 2005, *[Snipers]* is a deft mixture of SF and mystery with some very sharp plotting, some nice twists, and a trio of compelling characters."
—*Booklist,* starred review, on *Snipers*

"Rusch is best known for her Retrieval Artist series, but occasionally she gives us a standalone gem like *Snipers*.... *Snipers* is a riveting suspense tale and a fine SF story—what more could we want?"
—*Analog* on *Snipers*

Also by

Kristine Kathryn Rusch

THE FAERIE JUSTICE SERIES

Show Trial (novella)
The War and After (short-story collection)

OTHER HISTORICAL FICTION

Hitler's Angel
Snipers
The Enemy Within
The Tower (novella)

THE WAR AND AFTER
Five Stories of Magic & Revenge

A FAERIE JUSTICE COLLECTION

KRISTINE KATHRYN RUSCH

*wmg*PUBLISHING

The War and After: Five Stories of Magic & Revenge

Copyright © 2015 Kristine Kathryn Rusch
Published 2015 by WMG Publishing
www.wmgpublishing.com
Cover art copyright © Philcold/Dreamstime
Book and cover design copyright © 2015 by WMG Publishing
Cover design by Allyson Longueira/WMG Publishing
ISBN-13: 978-0-615-83912-7
ISBN-10: 0-615-83912-6

"Corpse Vision" by Kristine Kathryn Rusch was first published in *Jim Baen's Universe*, December 2009.

"Dark Corners" by Kristine Kathryn Rusch was first published in *Jim Baen's Universe*, 2007.

"Subtle Interpretations," was first published in *Mystery Date*, edited by Denise Little, Daw Books, February, 2008.

"Judgment," was first published in *Faerie Tales*, edited by Martin H. Greenberg and Russell Davis, Daw Books, May 2004.

"The Thrill of the Hunt" by Kristine Kathryn Rusch was first published in *Jim Baen's Universe*, February 2010.

Contents

THE WAR AND AFTER
Five Stories of Magic & Revenge

A FAERIE JUSTICE COLLECTION

Introduction

WAR HAUNTS ME. I don't know why. I've written about war for my entire career. From the books of the Fey to *Hitler's Angel*, I have examined war without being any clearer about what it means to me.

After I write this introduction, I'm starting a novella (short novel) called *Show Trial*, set during the Nuremberg trials. I've been planning this piece for a long time. It made itself known as I was writing two of the stories in this book. I needed to review those stories, so I figured now was the time to put them in a collection.

I have a lot of World War II stories. I'll collect more of them as time goes on. Most of them aren't stories that happen during the war. Most of them are about the impending war or the results of the war. Only one story in this volume is set during the fighting. Three of the others happen after the war, and one foreshadows the nightmares to come.

In this collection, I've done something I don't normally do: I've put the stories in chronological order. Not the order in which I wrote them. (If that was the case, then "Dark Corners" would come first.) The chronology here is history's chronology.

"Corpse Vision" comes first. Set in Paris in the 1920s, it hints at the horrors ahead. "Dark Corners," also set in Paris but this time in 1944, comes next. Both stories come from a trip I took to Paris in 2001. Laura Resnick and I went into the catacombs beneath the city, and learned that the resistance used that as one of their hiding places. I was both uncomfortable and intrigued, emotions that always lead me to research and then to storytelling.

"Subtle Interpretations" is the other Paris story of the volume, but this time, Paris is accidental: the language division of the U.S. Army, working for the Nuremberg Trials after the war, actually recruited out of the Paris International Telephone Exchange. I set this story in Paris because I had no real choice.

"Judgment" takes place in Nuremberg itself during the trials in 1945. I call these stories "practice" stories, not because I plan to rewrite them, but because they're messages from my subconscious, exploring areas that might or might not be in a larger work. Both stories stand alone, and neither will be part of the larger work—exactly, anyway—although bits and pieces will factor in.

Finally, "The Thrill of the Hunt" takes place in the 1950s. Various organizations did hunt escaped Nazis and, it's rumored, some organizations actually murdered the Nazis they found. That fact served as the impetus for the piece.

The stories here are dark—how can they not be?—but they're also cathartic, at least for me. They explore a dark period of human history, one we're lucky to have survived.

—Kristine Kathryn Rusch
Lincoln City, Oregon
January 8, 2011

Corpse Vision

*J*OE DECKER couldn't remember who poured him into the taxi that brought him to Le Café du Dôme. Either way, it had to be one of the Midwestern boys—gangly Jim Thurber or the new guy—whatsisname? William?—Shirer. Neither of them knew Decker had a room at the Hôtel de Lisbonne—him and everybody else at the *Trib* except that old stick Waverly Root. Of course, without that old stick, the paper wouldn't get out everyday for the ex-pats and tourists to read in their little Left Bank cafes. Some were saying—mostly the folks over at the *Paris Herald*—that an alcoholic wave was sweeping through the offices of the *Paris Tribune*, making it damned impossible to get anything out let alone a daily paper.

Like the deadbeats at the *Herald* could talk. What they said about the *Trib* applied to the *Herald* as well: Each and every day, a goodly proportion of the staff was insensate due to drink—half because it was there and half because it wasn't.

Joe Decker didn't drink when he worked. He drank after he worked, and then only because he didn't want to face his typewriter in that little room off Boulevard St. Michel. If anyone had told him he'd be writing hack in Paris while he was supposed to be writing his brilliant first novel, he would've laughed.

He'd come to Paris with $300, his typewriter, and a one tiny suitcase of clothes, figuring that, with the franc worth damn near nothing against the dollar, he could afford one year, one year of typing, one year of thinking, thinking, thinking. Six months later, he had 5,000 words of unadulterated horseshit and fifty dollars, barely enough to pay for the room which he was heartily sick of.

Besides, no one in Paris had heard of Prohibition or if they had, they thought it one of those crazy American ideas that would never work.

Oh yeah sure, it would never work. It had never worked him into a huge thirst, which he tried to slack on nights like this when he'd turned in his copy on some stupid tourist gala no one here gave a good goddamn about but which actually got sent home because the folks back at their parent paper, the *Chicago Tribune*, thought such things were the important goings-on in Paris.

He remembered heading down the twisty back stairs of the *Trib* building, the presses thudding, the air hot with fresh ink. Funny man Thurber had come along and What-sisname Shirer, still all googly eyed because he hadn't seen anything like this back in Ioway or Illanoise or wherever the hell he was from, and they'd planned one drink, just one—and the next thing Decker knew he woke up in this taxi with a throbbing headache and a mouth that tasted of three-day old gin.

In his exceedingly bad French, he'd asked the cabby where they were going. The cabby just waved his hand imperiously and said, "Le Dôme, Le Dôme," and Decker wasn't sure they were heading to the Dôme because Thurber or Whatsisname had told the cabby to go there, or because the cabby, like every other French taxi driver, knew the Dôme was the place to take drunk Americans so that they could get home.

Decker's head was too fuzzy to conjure the words to get the taxi to the Hôtel de Lisbonne. Besides, he wasn't sure he had the scratch. The ride to the Dôme was gratis—or would be if he couldn't find a franc or two—because someone there would cover the fare, if not one of the patrons then one of the uniformed police officers who paced the beat near the taxi stand.

He would have to promise to pay them back. And he would pay them back. He had paid everyone back, which was about the only good thing he could say about himself at the moment.

Nothing he did was any damn good, not even the daily copy he wrote for the *Trib*. The words were fine, the prose was solid, the assignments stank. His friends were just as miserable as he was (although, as Wave Root said, miserable in Paris is like happy everywhere else), and there wasn't even a woman in the picture. Well, not a relationship woman. There'd been more than Decker's fare share of one-night women. He might have even had one tonight.

The thought made him search his pockets as the taxi pulled up on the Rue Delambre side of the Dôme. The café had been on this corner for nearly thirty years, but only since the War had it become a haven for Americans. Know-it-all Hemingway, the only one of Decker's acquaintances who had finished his novel after he arrived in Paris, called it one of the three principal cafes in the Quarter, and the only one filled with people who worked.

No one who worked was there now. The tables on the terrace were empty, the chairs pushed out expectantly. A glow fell across them from the café's open doors.

Decker staggered out of the taxi, handed the driver the lone franc he'd found in his front pocket, and had to grip the pole marking the taxi stand to keep from falling.

Not only did he have a throbbing headache, but wobbly legs as well. He had to stop drinking, that was all there was to it.

"Coffee?"

Decker still had one arm wrapped around the pole. He thought maybe the ubiquitous uniformed policeman had spoken to him, but he didn't see an ubiquitous uniformed policeman. Instead, he saw an elderly man sitting against the wall, beneath the awning that someone should have rolled up by now.

"Or are you one of those British gentlemen who prefer tea?"

The old man spoke the oddly clipped English that Parisians learned—not quite British upper-class, but not quite British lower class either. Continental English, Root called it. Incontinent English, Thurber always amended when Root had left the room.

"Water would probably help," Decker said, not sure he should let go of the pole.

"Water *will* help. Alcohol dehydrates the system. That is half of what causes the so-called hang over."

The old man put a deliberate space between "hang" and "over." It was those kinds of errors that Decker usually found funny. The French often mangled English idioms, like the time the editor at *Le Petit Journal* had introduced Decker to his assistant, calling the man "my left hand"— and not meaning it as any kind of joke.

"*Monsieur,*" the old man said with a wave of a hand. "*Une bouteille d'eau.*"

Decker was going to tell him that the waiters here never showed up when you wanted them, and certainly wouldn't show when there were only a few customers, but the waiter who appeared, happily prying the top off a bottle of water, contradicted his very thought.

Of course, the old man wasn't just French. He had to be a regular. French regulars were prized at places like this, places which the Americans had taken over, like they had taken over most of Montparnasse just south of the Luxembourg Gardens. It was essentially an extension of the Latin Quarter without being in the Latin Quarter at all. It had been that way since the 16th century when Catherine de Medici had expelled students from the university. They had set up shop here and called it Montparnasse.

Decker knew such things about Paris, indeed, he had become a font of Paris trivia in his two years at the *Tribune*, all learned with bad schoolboy French and only a modicum of charm.

"It would be nice if you joined me," the old man said to Decker as the waiter put down the empty bottle and a single, rather grimy glass.

"Easier said than done," Decker said, not certain he could let go of the pole and remain standing.

The old man had a croissant in front of him and, despite the hour, a cup of coffee. He wore a proper black suit but no hat, which looked odd in the thin light. His hair was a yellowish white, speaking of too many hours in cafes around cigarette smoke.

As Decker lurched closer, using tables and the occasional chair to maintain his balance, he realized that the old man's beard was yellowish brown around his mouth. His fingers were tobacco stained as well. But he held no pipe and no cigar or cigarette had burned to ash in the tray in the center of the table.

Decker made it to the table and sank into the chair the old man had pushed back for him. It groaned beneath his weight. He tugged his suit coat over his stained white shirt. He had to look as filthy as he felt.

The old man poured water into the glass. The water looked clear and fresh despite the fingerprints on the side of the glass.

"You are an American newspaper man, yes?" the old man asked.

"Yes," Decker said, not that it was a hard guess, given their location.

"Joseph Decker, the American newspaper man, yes?" the old man said.

It gave Decker a start that the old man knew his name. "Is there another Joe Decker in Paris?"

The old man ignored the question. " "I have a story for you, should you take it."

Everyone had a story for him. Usually it was the kind of thing tourist rumors were made of, like why there were no fish in the Seine. But the old man didn't look like someone who would give Decker a song and dance.

Of course, Decker wasn't yet sober, so he had to assume his judgment about all things—like the kind of man the old man was based on how he appeared—was probably flawed.

"It's two a.m.," Decker said, "and—"

"Three a.m.," the old man said.

"Three a.m.," Decker said with a flash of irritation, "and I'm drunk. If you're serious about this story thing, we'll meet here tomorrow when I've had a chance to sleep this off, and we can talk then."

"I do not go out in the daylight," the old man said.

Two years ago, Decker would have rolled his eyes. But by now, he'd seen and heard everything. There were guys on the copy desk who didn't go out in the daylight either, saying it hurt their precious eyes.

Decker went out too much in the daylight, seeing things that sometimes he wished he hadn't.

He flashed on her then, body crumpled beneath Pont Neuf, feet dangling over the edge of the walkway along the banks of the Seine, pointing toward the river.

He closed his eyes and willed the image away.

"And that is why I do not," the old man said. "You see them too."

Decker opened his eyes. The old man was staring at him. The old man's eyes were blue and clear, not rheumy like Decker had expected. Maybe the old man was younger than Decker thought. He'd met a number of those guys in Paris—men in their forties who could pass for someone in their eighties by their clothing, their white hair, and their gait.

"I don't see anything, old man," Decker said.

"Nonsense," the old man said. "It is why you drink."

"I drink because I'm lonely," Decker said. *Because he kept writing the beginning to that damn novel over and over while Know-it-all Hemingway sat in this very café with his stupid notebook and scribbled story after story, book after book. Decker drank because he hated writing puff pieces for the folks back home, puff pieces about touristy restaurants and American musicians and writers like Know-it-all Hemingway. Decker drank because the stories he wanted to cover "would discourage the tourist trade from coming here." He drank because Paris wasn't the answer after all.*

"You drink," the old man said, "because it closes your mind's eye. I have watched you. You see too much."

"You've *watched* me?" Decker was getting more and more sober by the minute. "You're following me?"

"If you recall," the old man said with the patience people reserve for drunks, fools, and children, "I arrived before you did. But I must confess that I have been waiting for you."

"Me and all the other American hacks," Decker said.

The old man smiled, revealing tobacco-stained teeth. The smile was friendlier than Decker expected. "Admittedly, you American hacks, as you say, are dozens of dimes—"

Decker winced.

"—but I, in truth, have been waiting for you."

Decker drank his water. It did clear his head, although he wasn't entirely sure he wanted his head cleared. "What's so special about me?"

"You see," the old man said again.

This time, Decker did roll his eyes. He drank the last of his water, and stood up. "Old man, I'm so damned drunk that this conversation isn't making sense. How about I meet you here tomorrow at midnight, and I promise to be sober. Then you can tell me your story."

"It is your story," the old man said.

"Whatever you say," Decker said, taking the bottle of water and heading north.

He had a hell of a walk—at least for an exhausted drunk. Normally he wouldn't have minded the jaunt up to the twisty little streets near the Sorbonne. The Hôtel de Lisbonne was on the corner of Rue Monsieur-le-Prince and Rue de Vaugirard. All he had to do was walk the Boulevard Saint-Michel toward the Seine and he'd be in his bed in no time.

But he usually avoided the Boulevard Saint-Michel. He avoided a lot streets in Paris, at least on foot. The old man was right; Decker saw things. But he usually attributed those things to drink or to too much imagination.

The soldiers he always saw marching through the Arc de Triomphe wore no uniforms he recognized. They marched in lock-step, their heads turned side to side as if they were little tin soldiers with moving parts.

But he didn't always see the soldiers there. Sometimes he saw a flag that he didn't recognize with a Fylfot in the middle. The Fylfot, an ancient elaborate cross, was supposed to ward off evil. But he somehow got the sense that the Fylfot itself—at least as used here—was the evil.

On the Boulevard Saint-Michel, he saw students rioting in the streets. The students were grubby creatures, with long hair and carrying signs that he did not understand. Sunshine shone on them, although he only saw them when it was dark.

Because of these visions, he studied Paris history, and found nothing that resembled any of it. The soldiers were unfamiliar, just like the flag, and the students too filthy to belong to any modern generation. He could dismiss such things as figments of his imagination.

But the woman—she had been real.

He had touched her, her skin cold and clammy and gray from the elements. Her eyes had been open and cloudy, her lips parted ever so slightly.

He had found her six months into his trip to Paris. Shortly after, he had wandered into the offices of the *Trib*, such as they were, and offered up his services.

Novelist, eh, kid? The man at the copy desk had asked.
Yessir.

You know how many novelists we get here, hoping for a few bucks? At least two a day. Sorry.

I have experience…

Those fateful words. *I have experience.* And he did. From his college newspaper to the *Milwaukee Journal*—yes, he had been a good Midwestern boy, once too, a boy who didn't like near beer. A boy who actually had dreams for himself.

Five thousand words of horseshit later, stories about the tourists (*Mr. and Mrs. Gladwell arrived this afternoon on a trip that has taken them from their home in Lincoln, Nebraska, to New York City through London, and now here, in Paris, where they are staying at the Ritz…*), stories about everything except the woman, crumpled beneath Pont Neuf.

Somehow he made it to the Hôtel de Lisbonne without seeing anyone, real or imaginary. The front desk was empty, so he reached over it and grabbed his key.

As he climbed the dark narrow stairs to his room, he heard a typewriter rat-a-tat-tatting. Someone was working on something, maybe a short story, maybe a novel, maybe a freelance piece for *Town and Country*.

He unlocked his room and stepped inside, then stared at his own typewriter, gathering dust beneath the room's only window. A piece of paper had been rolled in the platen since sometime last month, with only a page number on the upper right hand corner (27), and a single lowercase word in the upper left.

…the…

As if it meant something. As if he knew what he was going to do with it.

The paper was probably ruined, forever curlicued, although it didn't matter. If he finished typing on that page, he could pile the other twenty-six pages on top of it, flattening it out.

If he sat down now, nearly sober, the old man's words still echoing in his head (*You see them too*), he would write:

The woman discarded at the foot of the bridge looked uncomfortably young. Her brown hair was falling out of Gibson Girl do, now horribly out of fashion, her lips painted a vivid red. Part of the lip rouge stained her front teeth. If she were alive, she would turn away from him, and surreptiously rub at that stain with her index finger.

He looked away from the typewriter, from that little accusatory "the." The description of the woman did not fit with the bucolic piece he had been writing, a memoir of Germantown Wisconsin in the days before the war, when he had been a young boy, and his father was still alive, tinkering with his new Model T, his mother tutting the dangers in the newfangled machinery, the bicycle he himself had built from a kit, with the help of the man who lived next door.

Those were the kind of books people read now, memories of times past, not bloody, dark stories about dead women on Paris streets.

Decker took off his suit and hung it up, although he didn't brush it out, like he should have. He lacked the energy.

As he pulled off his shirt, he realized the stains were worse than he had thought. Long, brown stains up front, looking like blood.

He was thinking of blood, though. He wasn't going to let his imagination win.

Besides, he still had one clean shirt. He needed to take the bundle to the laundry, along with his suit, so that he could look pressed and sharp again, instead of rumpled and disreputable.

He left his undershirt, boxers, and socks on, and tumbled onto the bed, the saggy mattress groaning beneath his weight. The bed hadn't even stopped bouncing by the time he had fallen asleep.

***

SHE WAS THERE IN HIS DREAMS, her rich brown hair piled on top of her head, with a few curls cascading around her face. She sat on the edge of the bridge, feet dangling over the Seine, leaning back toward the road. Her eyes smiled, her lips—a perfect cupid's bow, just like the drawings she mimicked—rouged darker than her cheeks. The makeup softened her living face, making her seem as unreal as the women in the advertisements.

While her hair was old-fashioned, her clothing was not. No buttoned down shirtwaist for her with a long skirt that fell to her ankles. She wore a black skirt that grazed her knees, silk stockings with a perfect line up the back, and a blouse so soft that it seemed almost indecent.

Around her neck, a simple St. Christopher's medal, and a delicate gold cross with a tiny diamond in the center. A gold band on her right hand, a band she twisted when she saw him approach, a frown creasing her lovely forehead.

He stopped beside her. She was American—he knew that without asking—and he held his reporter's notebook in his left hand, a pen in his right.

Her face shut down when he asked her name. And then her eyes clouded over, and her mouth opened ever so slightly.

The St. Christopher's medal disappeared and the gold ring too. But the expensive necklace, the gold cross with a diamond in the center, remained, as if it were her calling card.

He woke up thinking about it, twisted to one side, the bottom of the cross bent slightly as if she had fallen on it against the stone walkway.

She had worn no stockings when he found her body, and the sensible shoes, made for walking in a strange city (he knew that as clearly as if she had told him) had been replaced by thin heels, the kind flappers wore with their knee-length dresses and opera-length pearls.

He woke up thinking of the difference between the smiling girl in his dreams and the dead woman on the walkway, her skin cold against his fingertips.

He stared at his typewriter, his fingers itching to finish that sentence.

…the…

The.

The woman discarded…

Discarded.

He got dressed, and stumbled out of his room, ostensibly searching for breakfast, but really on his way to get another drink.

***

STILL, THAT DAY, he made it to midnight without taking a nip from the bottle he kept at the bottom of his desk drawer. He didn't take the glass of wine offered with dinner, nor did he drink the shot of vodka offered to him by the White Russian he'd met while waiting for the American tourists he was supposed to interview in Le Procope.

He arrived at the Dôme exactly at midnight, sober as a judge. Decker had pressed his suit and worn his last clean shirt, mostly as an apology for the way he had looked the night before.

He hadn't examined himself in the mirror until this morning, but even then he had looked a fright—his hair standing on end, his nose bulbous, the capillaries in his cheeks bursting from too much drink. His eyes were red rimmed and he knew his breath was bad enough to kill any small rodent unfortunate enough to cross his path.

So he cleaned up, although no one at the *Trib* noticed, except Whatsisname Shirer, the kid from Ioway or Illanoise. Whatsisname Shirer had raised his eyebrows, but hadn't made a single remark, smart ass or otherwise, and so no one else seemed to notice.

Thurber was busy making up the news. Root was working, trying to get someone at the copy desk to expand the notes his so-called reporters had turned in. Most everyone else was so bleary-eyed that they would think they were imagining Decker in his spiffed up clothes and slicked-back hair.

Alcoholic wave indeed. It had become an alcoholic ocean, and he was seeing it for the very first time.

The Dôme had customers this night, at least a dozen sitting on the terrace, with more inside. The interior was grayish blue from all the cigarette smoke—it looked like a fog had blown through Paris and gotten stuck only inside the Dôme.

Outside, a group of men crowded around one of the tables. Decker recognized some of them from the *transatlantic review*. They spoke earnestly to each other, one of them shaking the stem of his pipe at a bespectacled man in an American felt hat.

Decker avoided them, just like he'd taken to avoiding Know-it-all Hemingway. Instead he circled to the other side of the terrace, near the taxi stand. This evening, one of the ubiquitous uniformed policemen paced, hands clasped behind his back.

The Dôme seemed normal, not like something out of a painting, the way it had the night before.

Because Decker was concentrating on its normality, he almost missed the old man, sitting at the same table, his back against the café's glass windows. Another man sat with him, younger, sharply French with his narrow face, black hair, and up-to-the-minute gabardine suit.

Decker wandered over toward them, as if they weren't his destination at all. When he reached the table, he pulled out the only other chair and sat.

"You're lucky I remembered," he said.

"I knew you would." The old man wore the same suit. His eyes were as clear as Decker had thought. "You have not had a drink."

Damn that incontinent English. Decker couldn't tell if the old man had asked a question or made a statement. "I told you I'd be sober. You told me you had story."

The younger man stared at Decker as if he thought he was rude. Maybe he was.

"I said, I had a story *for you*." The old man emphasized the last two words.

Decker looked at the younger man. "Maybe some introductions would be a good place to start."

"Maybe not," the old man said. "We shall perform the—how do you say?—niceties after we have determined what disturbs you the most."

"What disturbs me the most," Decker said, "are people who waste my time."

He shoved the chair back, about to stand, when the old man touched his arm. The old man's skin was cold. In spite of himself, Decker shivered.

"Americans are impulsive," the old man said to his companion. "And somehow they have come to embrace a lack of politeness as if it is a virtue."

"Look," Decker said, almost adding "old man" like he had done last night when he was drunk. That had been rude, but not intentionally rude. "I deal in hard, cold facts. The first hard cold fact you learn about damn near anybody is his name, which you're not willing to tell me. So I'm not willing to stick around. See ya, pal."

This time he did stand. He was going to repeat the same walk he'd made the night before, up the Boulevard Saint-Michel. Maybe he should walk around the Luxembourg Gardens instead, meander instead of go directly.

He was nearly to the group of *transatlantic review* writers when the old man said, "The students, they will be in the street tonight. And tomorrow, the flag will fly over the Arc de Triomphe."

Decker stopped in spite of himself. A shiver ran down his spine. He hadn't told anyone about those waking dreams. Not even when he was drunk. Probably not even when he was black-out drunk, since he got quieter and quieter—a man who knew how to keep secrets, Root used to say, when he was the one who poured Decker into a taxi.

Decker pivoted. He walked back to the table, as the old man had known he would. But the old man did not smile like a man who had won an argument. Instead, he remained grimly serious. The younger man continued to stare.

"The soldiers leaning out of the Hôtel de Ville, do you not notice how blond they are?" The old man's voice was soft.

The other man watched Decker avidly, as if everything depended on his response.

The Hôtel de Ville was Paris's city hall. And he'd only seen soldiers there once, in the middle of a summer afternoon, as heat shimmered on the boulevards and he sat outside, trying to find a bit of air in a city not used to extreme warmth.

"They wore helmets," Decker said, knowing that was an admission.

"But they were fair-skinned, no?"

"Stocky," he said, wishing he hadn't responded. But that was what he had noticed, how stocky and square they were, as if the uniforms they wore with their unrecognizable helmets made them as solid as a boxer in the beer halls near Milwaukee.

"And they wore this symbol on their arms." The old man pushed a piece of paper forward with a Fylfot drawn on it.

In spite of himself, Decker sat back down. "Who are they?"

"A nightmare," the old man said. "One we pray we will not have. But our prayers will be for nothing. Because only strong nightmares leach backwards."

"Backwards?" Decker asked, thinking of the woman. Was that a backwards nightmare? He had seen her six months after he arrived—years ago now—and he dreamt of her every night, awakening from those dreams unsettled.

"The soldiers," the old man said. "They are little boys now, playing with battered tin soldiers from before the War. If, indeed, they are healthy enough to play. Most are hungry. Some are starving."

Decker frowned. Even when he was sober, Decker didn't understand the old man. The old man spoke nonsense. But a nonsense that Decker found enticing, in spite of himself.

"Starving?" Decker said. "Then why don't you do something?"

"Why don't you?" the old man asked. "Your country pushed for reparations. Your President Wilson. Somehow he knew how to cure the world. He made it sicker."

"Congress never ratified that treaty," Decker said, wondering why they were talking about the Treaty of Versailles conference from six years ago, from before he even arrived in the City of Light.

"And that makes it all better, no?" the old man said. "Leadership provided by your president here in Paris failed at home, so the fact that the other countries—"

"*Grand-père,*" the young man said, touching the old man's arm. "That is enough. He is not responsible for his country's follies."

"They are all responsible," the old man said.

Decker was frowning now.

"You were telling me about soldiers and little boys," Decker said, trying to get past this confusion. "Soldiers, little boys, and backwards nightmares."

"They are not nightmares," the younger man said. "They are visions. The future, haunting us here and now."

Decker frowned. "The future?"

The young man nodded. "Events so powerful they reach backwards to us. We have seen the soldiers for generations now. We have not understood them until— what is it you call it?—the Peace of Paris."

"You understand it now?" Decker asked.

"We understand that they are Germans."

24

"Marching into Paris." Decker snorted. "Are you hoping for this?"

Three men from nearby tables stared. Most everyone here served in the War or had lost someone who had.

"No," the younger man said, holding up his hands. "It is the worst kind of tragedy. But we do know, from the students who are also a vision leaching backwards, that Paris herself will stand."

"The students." Decker wasn't going to ask any more and he wasn't going to reveal what he had seen. He was assuming the younger man meant the grubby students he had seen some nights as he walked up the Boulevard Saint-Michel.

"Saint-Sulpice stands. Notre Dame stands. Le Tour Eiffel stands. In the distance, away from the shouting, you can see Le Sacré-Coeur. The bridges remain. If the Germans were to destroy Paris, they would bomb the bridges so that no army could follow. Then they would destroy the monuments to destroy our souls."

Decker couldn't resist any longer. "How do you know the students appear later?"

"They are less solid."

"You can't touch them?" Decker asked.

"No," the younger man said. "You have not tried?"

He had avoided everything. He had avoided the students and the soldiers and the flags. He heard the whispery voices, and figured they had come from his own drunkenness.

"Can you touch current nightmares?" Decker asked.

"Only reality," the old man said.

Her skin, cold against Decker's fingers. So she *had* been real. Had he spoken to her once? Holding his notebook? Wanting to know who she was?

Why would he have spoken to her? He wasn't yet working for the *Trib*. He was playing at being a famous writer, the American James Joyce, yet to publish his *Portrait of the Artist As a Young Man*.

"Ah," the old man said, peering into Decker's face. "Something precipitated your visions. You did not see them when you first came to Paris."

Decker looked at him. The old man's skin was papery thin, his eyebrows so bushy they seemed to grow toward his scalp.

Paris had been clean. Paris had been pure. Truly the City of Light, all beauty and glistening stone, history calling to him.

Not like Milwaukee. Milwaukee had turned dark, especially near the lakefront. He had seen corpses of sailors, washed against the rocks, their uniforms still sodden with the waters of Lake Michigan. He had screamed the first time, and people had run to him, not to them, not even when he pointed....

He shook his head. He did not want to think of this. He did not want to remember it, how each street had something, someone, who sprawled along a road or had been shot on apartment steps or had been squashed flat by a new-fangled motorcar.

Sometimes two, sometimes three per block. He had walked with his eyes closed, and his mother—his beautiful tiny mother—whispering that he had to do something else, something that took him away from death.

Write your novel, she had said. *I will tell people of my son, the famous writer.*

And she had given him all of her pin money, money he knew she relied upon to get away from his father.

His father, who drank.

"What was that precipitated these visions?" the old man asked. "A drink, perhaps. You like your drink."

Decker stared at him, feeling his gaze go flat with anger.

"No, it could not be drink," the younger man said. "Or he wouldn't continue drinking. It's got to be hereditary. Let me see your hands."

Decker closed his hands into fists. He didn't want these people to touch him. He looked at the old man.

"You said you had a story for me."

"I have a city of stories, if you're willing to listen," the old man said. "But first, we must see the root of your vision."

Decker stared at him, then slowly, reluctantly, extended his right hand.

***

HE HAD FIRST SEEN HER on the Champs Elysées, a vision in white. She looked like the old world blending with the new, her Gibson Girl hairdo, the wide-brimmed hat (with ribbons trailing it) that she carried in her left hand. Her dress was narrow, with a flip just near the knees, her stockings perfect, her shoes solid, old-fashioned, buttoned-up leather.

He had seen no Parisians woman dressed like that—mixing styles. Parisian women had their own style, a lot more fluid, a lot more suggestive, and all of them wore cloche hats (if they wore hats at all). She smiled when she saw him, a broad, wide American smile, the kind that held nothing back.

He tipped his hat to her. She laughed and continued onward as if she had known they would see each other again.

Of course they had. She had been looking at the sights, such a tourist, and he had been moving from park bench to park bench, staring at the monuments.

He had talked with her on Pont Neuf, more than once. She had laughed and flirted and never once told him her name. No one seemed to want to tell him names.

The thought disconcerted him for a moment, and the image of her laughing face wavered. He heard voices all around him, male voices mostly, and the air filled with tobacco smoke. An old man was peering at the palm of his hand as if it held the secrets of the universe.

And then she was back, looking at him sideways. She was holding his hand, palm up, as if she could see his future in it. She was young, enjoying Paris. He hadn't enjoyed Paris until her. Not like this—climbing the Eiffel Tower and going to Versailles to see the gardens, wandering through the Louvre, and eating bread and cheese for lunch in the Tuileries.

And he wrote. How he wrote. The novel, abandoned, he didn't care about Lincoln. He wrote instead about—

...the woman, discarded, like abandoned laundry at the base of the bridge. Her killer, dark, darker than anything Edgar Allan Poe could imagine in his darkest Rue Morgue

dreams. The man carried her from the bridge itself, down the side, preparing to dump her in the Seine when someone called out...

He looked up, saw the younger man staring at him with something like horror, the old man with eyes full of compassion.

"Corpse Vision," the young man said. "You have Corpse Vision."

***

DECKER WASN'T SURE he wanted them to tell him what Corpse Vision was, although he had a hunch he knew.

The memories scrolled backwards—like the nightmares the old man had mentioned—the first homicide call on the police beat, near one of the speakeasies by the lakefront. The dead man wore spats and a snazzy hat that blew toward Decker in the wind. He caught the hat, knew enough to carry it back to the detective, and as he did, his foot brushed the corpse, his ankle actually hitting the dead man's elbow.

A little bit of nothing—a bit of a shiver, a bit of a chill—but not much more until he returned to the *Journal's* city room. He found a typewriter and banged out his recollections, handing the paper to the copy desk for expansion. He went back to the desk to type a few impressions, like he used to do, for the novels he would someday write. But first, he rested his cheek on his fist and closed his eyes.

Spats rose from the sand, backwards, like a Charlie Chaplin film being rewound, shaking his fist at someone near on the docks. A flash of a knife, a dropped bottle of gin, some money clanging against the wood, and Decker opened his eyes, terrified of his waking dream.

The next morning, he went to the lakefront as follow-up, at least that was what he told himself, and instead, he saw the sailors, washed up on the rocks, the air cold off Lake Michigan, and two little boys, standing in the middle of the corpses, fishing.

That was when Decker screamed. The last time he screamed when he saw a corpse.

But not the first time.

The first time—Lord, he'd been ten. On his grandfather's farm. His father had come back from the stream, looking grim, the female barn cat following him, crying plaintively. Decker should have followed his father, but he was already afraid of the man. So he went to the stream, saw the tiny kitten corpse on one of the rocks, touched it—the cold damp fur—and turned.

The man behind him had no eyes. He was tied to a tree, his skin filled with holes, birds sitting on his shoulders and pecking at his face.

Decker had screamed and screamed. His father had come first, pulled him away, told him he was a baby—he knew it was spring and every spring, his grandfather took the pick of the litter for barn cats and drowned the rest so the farm didn't get overrun with cats.

Someday, his dad had said grimly, *this'll be your job.*

But Decker only dimly heard the words. Instead, he stared at the dead man tied to the tree, the birds taking chunks out of his face as if he were a particularly delectable roast. Decker wanted to bury his own face in his dad's chest, but he knew better.

He also knew he needed to gather himself, to stop being so upset, but he couldn't. He couldn't. He sobbed and sobbed and finally his dad picked him up like a sack of potatoes and slung him over his shoulder, carrying him back, Decker hiccoughing, his father whacking his butt with every single hitched breath.

His mother came into his room that night when he screamed again, the dead man alive in his room as a vision, running from men Decker dimly recognized. They would catch the dead man, carve him up, tie him to the tree, and laugh when they told him the birds would get him. They laughed. And Decker recognized the laughs.

But that wasn't why he screamed. He screamed at the sunlight afternoon invading his dark room, the trees no longer there leading down to the stream, the bank where he'd happily played just a few years before.

His mother had come and shushed him. She had cradled him as if he were still a baby, and rocked him, but she said nothing.

Except when she thought he was asleep, she went back to the room she shared with his father—*You promised,* she said.

I did not send him down there, his father said. *He went on his own.*

You should have watched him.

You coddle him.

He doesn't need to see.

At his age, I was drowning kittens. I had killed chickens and butchered pigs. I fished. You deny him childhood.

That isn't childhood, she said. *See what it has done to you.*

You used to love me, his father said.

Before the darkness ate you, she said. *Before it ate you alive.*

***

"You could spend your whole life in escape," the old man said, again misusing idioms. It was the odd choice of words that brought Decker back to the Dôme, not the fact that he wanted to be back.

The men from the *transatlantic review* had left. In their place, a group from the *Herald*. One of the reporters tipped his hat to Decker, who nodded. He couldn't for the life of him think of the man's name.

"Each place will be new and fresh until death," the old man said. "Then you will see—and in Europe, there is much death to see."

"I'm not seeing corpses," Decker said before he could stop himself. Not that he admitted anyway. He drank too much to remember what he saw. And what he did remember the old man called backwards nightmares.

"You are not looking," the old man said. "You have deliberately blinded your most important eye."

Decker was getting a headache, and he was starting to wish for a drink. This had been a mistake. He didn't like being sober, not any more.

"You lied," Decker said. "You said you had a story for me. This whole meeting has been nothing but gibberish."

He stood, conscious of how odd he felt. He didn't want to be near these men. He didn't want to be at the Dôme. He wanted to talk to his mother, and she was thousands of miles away, probably worrying about him, like she did. She worried.

She thought he could outrun the family curse. The old man just said he couldn't.

Decker didn't want to think about any of it.

"We will be here tomorrow night," the old man said.

"I won't," Decker said.

"Unless you finish the story," said the younger man.

"We would love to read it," the old man said.

"Sure," Decker said. And he would love to start over, that fresh bright attitude he had brought to Paris so far gone that he couldn't even remember how it felt.

Maybe he could recapture it somewhere else. He had heard nice things about Vienna. There was another sister paper in Geneva—or maybe that was a sister to the *Herald*. United Press operated out of most countries.

He could leave in the morning. He didn't need the language skills. He hadn't had all that many in France. Besides, French was the language of diplomacy. He spoke it just badly enough for people to take pity on him.

He was going to go speak it badly now at the nearest bar he could find. He would speak it until he couldn't talk any more, until he didn't think about all the things the old man had brought back into his mind. He would be so bleary-eyed drunk that maybe he wouldn't even dream.

***

BUT HE MADE the mistake of stopping in his room first. He wanted more cash, which he found rolled up in his socks in the bottom drawer of the shabby bureau. Anyone would know to look in the sock drawer for money. It was a testament to how honest the staff was at the Hôtel de Lisbonne that no one had stolen his stash.

How honest or how lax. He couldn't remember the last time they cleaned his room.

He wiped a finger over the typewriter, removing dust. His eye caught the edge of that paper.

…the…

He sat down, xxed out the "the," and typed:

Sophie Nance Brown, daughter of Mr. and Mrs. Harcourt Brown lately of Newport, Rhode Island, in what the police initially reported as a bungled suicide attempt.

(Although, he thought, how could it have been bungled if she did indeed die?)

The body, discovered by an American tourist, fell on the walkway beneath the Pont Neuf. A witness claimed she had jumped off the bridge's wide stone railing, laughing as she fell.

But the American tourist contradicted these things, saying no one could have seen her fall. He found her at 7 a.m. Any witnesses would have had to been on the bridge in the middle of the night.

The American also pointed to her missing stockings and mismatched shoes. Her traveling companion, one Eleanor Rose Stockdale of Battle Creek, Michigan, said Miss Brown had never traveled anywhere without her St. Christopher's medal and her grandmother's solid gold wedding ring, both missing.

Police now believe Sophie Nance Brown is the third victim of a killer who play tricks on investigating officers. The witness who claimed she had fallen matched the description of a man seen carrying an unconscious woman to the base of the bridge around midnight.

Anyone with information about this most interesting case should contact the Prefect of Police.

Decker stared at the words. The paper did indeed come out of the platen curled, but he didn't care. The story was good enough for the *Trib*, if it published crime news like that (which it did not, afraid it would scare the tourists). But the story wasn't really good, just good enough.

He had written the facts as he had been trained. But that wasn't what he *knew*.

What he knew was this:

The woman discarded at the foot of the bridge looked uncomfortably young. Her brown hair was falling out of Gibson Girl do, now horribly out of fashion, her lips painted a vivid red. Part of the lip rouge stained her front teeth. If she were alive, she would turn away from him, and surreptitiously rub at that stain with her index finger.

She *had* turned away from him and wiped at the stain, the very first time she had seen him. Sophie Nance Brown, of Newport and Westchester and points south. Sophie Nance Brown with the laughing eyes, who said she had come to Paris for the *adventure.*

But her index finger was broken, bent backwards at an angle painful to look at, even now, when he knew she could feel nothing.

She had felt something. She had felt too much something when she went to the bridge after a long dinner on the Right Bank with friends. She wanted to feel the breeze in her hair, look at the moonlight over the Seine. She asked her traveling companion, Eleanor Rose Stockdale of Battle Creek, Michigan, to accompany her, but Eleanor Rose, a sensible girl, had heard that nice people did not stand on the bridges at night and had declined.

Later, Miss Stockdale would say she thought saying such things would discourage Miss Brown, but other friends said nothing discouraged Miss Brown when she set her mind to something.

Miss Brown had met a young man who had captured her fancy. Her interest in him was what she wanted to discuss with her friends at dinner. Knowing him had caused an ethical dilemma for her, especially since she was so far from home. He lived alone in a solitary room in one of the more disreputable hotels near the Sorbonne.

Miss Brown worried that she was too old-fashioned for the new morality, but too young to press the young man into something less exciting, something more permanent.

Instead of listening to her, Miss Brown's friends teased her "mercilessly." They laughed their way through dinner, interrupting her, until she grew angry, threw down her napkin along with a few francs and left the restaurant, heading for the Pont Neuf.

The Pont Neuf was suggestive, Miss Stockdale said, because Miss Brown found it romantic.

Miss Brown stood in the center of the bridge, peer out over the Seine at the famed lights of Paris, thinking that no woman should stand in such a spot alone. The light played with her old-fashioned hairstyle and her modern clothing, her ankles nicely turned out, the skirt accenting her shapely legs.

He had noticed that. He had noticed the contradiction from the start.

Decker paused, his wrists aching. He had them bent at an odd angle. His headache had cleared for the first time since he started drinking in Paris.

He wasn't writing news any longer—or at least, he wasn't writing news that he recognized. He was writing something else, *seeing* something else, something he didn't want to think about.

The pages had piled up on the small desk beside his typewriter. The voice was odd. It wasn't his, and it wasn't exactly the voice of impartial journalist. He was edging into something else, something his editors would disapprove of—"worried" and "thinking" and "noticing"—actual viewpoints, which were not allowed in the dispassionate prose of journalism.

Decker rolled another sheet of paper in the platen, ready to type that damning "the" again, ready to leave it, and count all of this as an aberration.

Instead, he continued:

> He had watched her since she got off the boat. She wore a wide brimmed hat with a red ribbon, fanciful and old-fashioned. Her clothing hinted at a girl who wanted to break out of the old ways, but her hair spoke of a girl who cherished what had come before.
>
> Almost Parisian. Modern, yet grounded in the past. He loved his city, and he wished others would as well. But he did not love the tourists, particularly the American ones, with their loud braying laughter and their lack of manners.

Although they grew their women tall and
beautiful in America. Solid women, with high
cheekbones and flashing eyes.

He followed her to her hotel, then watched
her, meeting her first on the Champs Elysées,
then finding her in the Tuileries, regaling her
with stories of his novel—every young man
in Paris these days had a novel—his notebook
clutched in his hand....

Decker stopped. Those memories, the things he saw,
they weren't his? He frowned, trying to see something else,
trying to remember when he had first met her. The date—

He dreamed of her. He dreamed of her, *after* he had
found her. Six months into his stay in Paris.

Six months.

But he had never seen her, touched her, laughed with
her. He hadn't really encountered her until he saw her
half-naked foot hanging off the walkway, her shoe dangling over the sparkling waters of the Seine.

Only it wasn't her shoe. The killer changed the shoes.
That was his little joke. He tossed her sensible shoes in the
water and gave her little Parisian heels, delicate shoes that
he had bought just for this purpose....

Not Decker. *Him*,

Etienne Netter, whose apartment in the
Seventh Arrondissement had been in his family for six decades. His parents long dead, his
mother distressed when he came home from
the War with "haunted eyes."

39

"But at least I am home, Mother," he said plaintively, when so many young men had not come home. She had not seen what he had seen, how the blood turned French fields into mud, all for the sake of a few meters of advancement that would probably be lost the following day.

They said the Americans changed it all, with their energy and their numbers and their willingness to get killed. The Americans, big and hearty, like their women, who were stupid but lucky and somehow managed to end the war.

They liked him, these American women. They thought him their pet Frenchman. They thought his accent "quaint," his smile "romantic," his desire to write novels "almost American," even though the French had been writing novels before America was a country.

He charmed them, relaxed them, promised them he would show them the sights—and he did. He did. He showed them their own venal faces in the Seine before he raised their skirts, ripped off their stockings, and proved to them that French men hadn't lost all of their dignity in the trenches.

His mother, before she died, said he had lost his soul on the battlefield, that he had come home a shell, not a man at all, filled with dark compulsions not French. She tried to take him to church, but he would not go, not even to her funeral, after she had died, stepping in front of one of the automobiles that she so despised for ruining the lovely streets of Paris.

Stepping—that is what he told the police. She had lost track of where she was in the conversation, and she had stepped—

But she had not stepped. She had stumbled, after a shove, after she called him a monster, and said she wished he had died on the battlefield along with his soul.

Sometimes he thought she was right. He had seen the darkness coming for him those early days in the woods, lurking beyond the tanks and the flying machines, past the machine guns with their rat-a-tat-tats and their spray of bullets, the bodies falling, falling, falling in the mud. Beyond that, the darkness rose over the fields and extended across Europe, and he saw it coming toward him, then filling him, until there was no room for anything else.

He could pass on the darkness—he had done so with that beautiful American—but as he watched the hope die in her eyes, he remembered how that felt, and he could not, he would not, let her live with that. So he took the life from her, knowing (although she did not know) that it was no longer worth living.

He had taken her St. Christopher's medal because it should not touch darkness. He had left the medal and the ring she wore in the poor box at Notre Dame. He did such things, venturing into churches only for that, then escaping before the darkness polluted them as well.

Sometimes he thought he should have stumbled in front of that automobile instead of sending his mother there. Sometimes he thought he should have died, just as she said, in the mud-and-blood soaked fields, along with his friends. Sometimes he thought.

And sometimes, he did not.

Decker could not look at what he had written. He stacked the paper inside one of his folders and tied it shut with a ribbon, just like he used to tie the pages of his novel inside the folder, proud of his day's work.

This day—this night—he was not proud. He was spent.

He had seen things he had hoped to never see again.

Corpse Vision, the old man's grandson had called it.

Whatever it was, Decker despised it, much as the man he had written about, this Etienne, had despised the darkness in himself.

***

As DECKER WALKED to the Dôme the following night, the folder under his arm, he saw the darkness lurking. It hid in the shadows, wearing uniforms he did not recognize—that symbol the grandson had drawn—marching in lock-step.

Nightmares seeping backwards.

But Etienne had been a nightmare seeping forward.

Decker winced. He did not want to think about it.

He hadn't had a drink in three days. His alcoholic wave was over.

He also hadn't been to the *Tribune* in three days. He wondered what Root would think, what Thurber would say. Maybe they were already searching for him, although no one had come to his room at the Hôtel de Lisbonne—or if they had, he had been too absorbed to hear their knock.

This time, Decker arrived before the old man. Decker sat at the old man's table, sipping coffee and eating ham, cheese, and bread, much to the disapproval of his waiter, who wanted to serve the coffee long after the meal was done.

Know-it-all Hemingway sat in a corner, scribbling in his journal. He did not look up as Decker came onto the terrace, and Decker did not call attention to himself.

But as he looked at Hemingway now, he saw something that startled him—an insecurity, a fear, so deep that Hemingway might not have known it existed. Superimposed over Hemingway—like a ghost in a Dadaist painting—was an old man with a white beard and haunted eyes. He hefted a shotgun and rubbed its barrel against his mouth.

Decker looked away.

The old man—his old man, not the spirit surrounding Hemingway—sat at the table, his grandson beside him.

Decker didn't ask where they came from. He didn't remark on their silent entrance. Instead, he handed the folder to the old man.

The old man untied the folder, opened it, and scanned the pages, handing them one by one to his grandson.

Decker read upside down, embarrassed by the words, their lack of cohesion, their meandering viewpoint. When the grandson saw the name Etienne Netter, he stood.

"My thanks," he said and bowed to Decker. Then he walked away, leaving the pages beside Decker's plate.

Decker did not touch them. The old man picked them up and put them back in the folder, which he tied shut, making a careful bow.

"It is more than I could have hoped for," he said. "You have saved lives."

Decker shook his head. "I didn't do anything."

"This man, this Netter, he is a new breed. You have heard of Jack the Red, no? Saucy Jack?"

"The Ripper," Decker said. "Decades ago. In London."

"The first of his kind, we think," the old man said. "If there had been one such as you, perhaps he would have been stopped."

"He was stopped," Decker said. "He only killed five."

"That we know of," the old man said.

He set the papers under his own plate, then extended his hand. "I am Pierre LeBeau. I run *Noir*, the central newspaper in the City of Dark."

Decker couldn't take the misstatements any more. "City of Light," he said. "We call Paris the City of Light."

LeBeau nodded. "Light has its opposite. You have seen the dark. You write of it. You know what is coming."

"Only because you tell me that it is," Decker said. He sipped his coffee, pleased that his hand remained steady. "How come I've never seen your paper?"

"As I have said, you kept your most important eye deliberately closed." LeBeau put his hand on top of the folder. "The paper has grown since the War. Before, we were a single sheet. During, we ran four. After, we grew to five, then ten, now eighteen. We need an English language edition. We will start with four pages on the expatriate community."

"More meeting the boat," Decker said. "More puff pieces."

"No puff, as you say," LeBeau said. "Warnings, perhaps. Stories that do not run in your *Tribune* or the *Herald*, things only hinted at in the fictions your friends write for the *transatlantic review*."

"Who would read it?" Decker asked, surprising himself. Normally he would ask about pay before readership.

"People like my grandson," LeBeau said.

"Where did he go?"

"He will take Etienne Netter and extinguish his darkness. Then he would help the police find justice."

"He'll kill him?"

"No," LeBeau said. "But this Netter might wish he were dead when my grandson has finished with this. For Netter will realize what he has done and why, and with the revival of his soul, he will feel remorse so painful that death will be the only way out. Yet death will be impossible for decades. It is our smallest but best measure of revenge."

Decker felt a chill run down his back. The conversations with LeBeau, as circular as they were, were beginning to make sense.

"We will pay triple what you earn at the *Tribune* for the first six months," LeBeau said. "Raises every quarter thereafter if you continue to perform."

"Perform?" Decker asked.

"You must follow the darkness," LeBeau said. "See where it will lead."

"And if I don't?"

LeBeau smiled. "I shall buy you your next drink. You will become one of the—what do they call it?—casualties of the licentiousness of Paris. There will be no novel, no more hack work as you call it, no more typing. Only drinks, until one day not even the drinks will work. You will go to a sanatorium, and they will try to help you, but you will be one of the hopeless ones, the ones who has rotted his mind and his body, but has not managed to destroy the vision that has haunted you since you touched that kitten decades ago."

It no longer surprised Decker that LeBeau knew so much about him. Nor did LeBeau's description of his future surprise him. Decker had seen it already, as his father drank more and more, until finally his grandfather drove his father away to "a hospital" where they would "help" him. No one had ever seen him again.

His mother would not speak of him. She had lived too close to his darkness. She feared it for her son.

But running from it hadn't worked. He had simply become a drunk in Paris instead of in Milwaukee. Even if he had no magic vision, he had a future like the one LeBeau had described.

And the writing had taken away the urge to drink.

Even if the things he wrote had chilled him deeper than anything else.

"I never met her, did I?" Decker asked the old man. "Sophie. I never did meet her."

LeBeau looked at him. "You met her. Her spirit, after she had died. She wished she had been with you instead of this Etienne. She used your similarities to pull you in. She wanted him stopped. She did not want him to harm anyone else."

It sounded good. Decker wasn't sure he believed it, but he wanted to. Just like he wanted to believe that *Noir* existed, that he would be paid three times his *Tribune* salary, that his Corpse Vision actually had a purpose.

"I suppose I can't tell anyone what I'm doing," he said.

LeBeau shrugged. "You can tell," he said. "They will not believe. Or worse, they will not care, any more than you care for them."

LeBeau glanced at Hemingway, still scribbling in his notebook. Decker looked too. Hemingway raised his head. For one moment, their eyes met. But Hemingway's were glazed, and Decker realized that Hemingway had not seen him, so lost was he in the world he was creating.

They were all creating their worlds. The expatriate reporters with their chummy newspapers in English, hiding in a French city that did not care about their small world. The novelists, sitting in Parisian cafes, writing about their families back home.

And the old man, with his darkness and nightmares looming backwards.

Decker already existed in darkness. He could no longer push it away. He might as well shine a light on it and see what he found underneath.

"I'll take four times the salary," he said, "and a raise every two months."

The old man smiled. "It is, as you say, a deal."

He extended his hand. Decker took it. It was dry and warm. They shook, and Decker felt remarkably calm.

Calmer than he had felt in months.

Maybe than he had felt in years.

He did not know how long *Noir* would be in his future. But he did know that his tenure there would be better than anything he had done in the past.

Anything he had seen in the past.

He opened his most important eye, and finally, went to work.

Dark Corners

*T*HE FIGHTING HAD been going on for days. Outbursts of gunfire—six German soldiers dead in front of the Gare d'Orsay—a full-scale battle, complete with barricades that the French love so much, near the Eiffel tower.

Solae had come to the surface because he heard the Resistance and the Germans had brokered a truce. The Resistance needed the time to organize, to wait for the Allies to arrive. The Germans, who were beginning to understand that they could not hold Paris, needed time to make a plan.

Solae needed food, so he had come to the only safe place he knew—a boulangerie on the Boulevard St. Germain. Most of the French were in hiding, not waiting in bread lines, and the Germans were at their posts.

He thought he would be able to slip in and out, unnoticed.

He had been wrong.

Solae ran across the boulevard, a loaf of bread beneath his arm, panic in his throat. He was thinner than most, so thin that if he turned sideways, the less observant could not see him. But he could not turn now.

The baker—a burly man who baked every morning for the Boche as if they were no different from the French he once served—was chasing Solae, shouting at the top of his lungs:

"Foul boy! Thief!"

Two storm troopers appeared from a kiosk, holding ripped posters telling Parisians to rise up against the Boche. The troopers looked ready for battle. They had shiny boots and shinier guns—and their eyes, that pale blue that the Boche seemed to worship—seemed even paler in the August sunlight.

Solae grabbed his bicycle, also stolen, and pedaled as fast as he could, praying that the troopers would not follow in a car. Was a bread thief worth the gas? Surely there were other battles to fight, other people to attack.

But he knew that the Germans—the filthy Boche—were like rabid dogs, unable to let go of anything once they sank their teeth into it.

He pedaled hard, weaving in and out of the bicycle traffic. Despite the fighting, Parisians were still on the streets, going about their business, ignoring the war as best they could, just like they had these last four years.

Behind him, he heard the roar of an engine. He glanced over his shoulder.

The troopers had followed him. Theirs was the only car on the boulevard. Their helmets made their heads look round and comical, but Solae did not laugh at them.

He had not laughed at the Boche for a long time, not since they put out the lights in his fair city. Not since his father's death.

Solae pedaled faster, but he could not stay ahead of the car. It roared behind him, and it would only be a moment before it caught him.

The bread was warm beneath his arm. Sweat ran down his face, and he wished, not for the first time, that he had the magic of his ancestors.

He would make the Boche vanish. He would explode them, destroy their vehicle, wipe their race from the earth.

But he could do none of these things. His people could do none of these things. The powers that had once belonged to faerie had faded centuries ago. When he was his most cynical, he believed that his people had had no great powers at all—that Faeryland and the magic that went with it were the myths the Real Ones believed them to be.

The Boche sitting on the right aimed his rifle at Solae, and Solae's breath caught. He imagined light streaming from his fingers, destroying the rifle, destroying the Boche.

But imagination did not make it so.

Instead, Solae veered onto a side street, then another, his bike bouncing on the cobblestones. He was near the entrance his people kept hidden with their tiny powers.

In one movement, he slipped off the bike and laid it against the closed and locked door of an empty shop. He gave the bike a longing glance—it had been by far the best bicycle he had stolen—and then he slipped sideways.

The Boche squeezed their vehicle onto the tiny street, the tires on the left side of the car riding on the curb. The Boche were laughing, calling out in German and bad French, promising le jeune a present if he but stopped for them.

Solae knew what kind of present they would give him: a bullet in the heart. And no amount of magic could undo that kind of damage.

The Boche did not seem to see him, even though one looked directly at him. Solae slipped around the corner and hid against a white wall covered with dead bougainvillea, until the Boche, their merriment gone, backed out of the street, and left him alone.

***

SOLAE HAD NOT ALWAYS stolen bread.

Once the Real Ones of Paris thought him the favored son of a nightclub owner, a man who specialized in acts that had a touch of glamour to them—be it the way a chanteuse's songs seemed to come alive on stage or the way that a young dancer almost seemed to fly as she leapt into the arms of her partner.

There had been magic during those nights. Not the magic of Solae's ancestors, but slighter magic, a bit of beauty that seemed to brighten the darkness.

Not that there had been much darkness then.

Less than a decade ago, when Solae was a little boy, he used to escape the smoke of his father's nightclub and climb onto the roof. There he looked at the lights of Paris—the arc lights illuminating the Eiffel tower, the gargoyles of Notre Dame grinning in the lights on the dome, the lights of Le Sacré-Coeur on top of Montemarte, glowing like candles in the distance.

The Real Ones called Paris La Ville Lumière, the City of Light. Perhaps they thought of the clear, crisp sunlight which, they said, they could not find anywhere else, but Solae always thought of the nighttime when the lights of the city made Paris as bright as day.

But when the bombings started, five years before—he had still been a boy then—the lights went out. Paris had not been La Ville Lumière for one-third of his life. It had become a place where darkness grew, like a hole in his soul.

For Solae, the absence of light was like the absence of air. His magic was not like his father's. The family already knew that Solae would not run the night club. Solae couldn't enhance acts, nor could he make a plain woman beautiful.

For a long time, his family thought he had no gifts at all.

And then they realized that his gifts were even subtler than usual—the ability to fade away in a crowd, or to brighten a room when he entered it.

Solae was not a creature of the night as so many of his kind were. He preferred the day, and if he had to chose a type of day, he preferred the bright sunlight of a Paris afternoon, the way the light fell upon the Seine, illuminating the classic lines of the Palace du Louvre and the magnificent windows of the Gare d'Orsay.

Sometimes Solae sat on the stone edge of the Pont Saint-Michel and watched the city pass him by, enjoying the light, the warmth, the way Parisians seemed to enjoy each moment.

He had not sat on the Pont Saint-Michel in four years, not since the Boche came in tanks, hanging their filthy flag with its ancient symbol, the swastika, across the Arc de Triomphe.

Usually, his people did not become involved in the ways of the Real Ones, except as his father did, to make money to survive. So many of faerie had moved to the city decades before. No one questioned strangeness in Paris. Even though it was a Catholic city in a Catholic country, certain behaviors were ignored.

Faerie who would have been hanged or shot or burned in the countryside were tolerated here. Many, like Solae's father, were more than tolerated.

They were loved.

And now they were gone. His father to a bullet in the middle of a piano medley. Stormtroopers, drunk with power, insisted on hearing "Ein Prosit" and Solae's father, who hated the Boche with a passion that made Solae's seem tepid, refused.

His father had railed against the Boche from the moment they began their campaigns in the Real Years of the 1930s. Remember, he said to his wife and sons, the Germans are the ones who exposed us, told our histories as if they were fables for children, made us less than we are.

And that night, the night the Germans wanted to hear "Ein Prosit," his father spoke of his hatred. The Boche reminded Solae's father that France was theirs now.

France belongs to no man, Solae's father said, his meaning clearer to faerie than it was to the Real Ones in the room. On some level, France had magic in her soul, magic that had been purged from so many European countries long ago.

Soon, the Boche told him, we shall remake France in our own image.

And you shall fail, Solae's father said, just as you failed to hear "Ein Prosit."

The words grew heated, and even Solae, who had been near the door, watching the lights of the city with a craving he still did not understand, turned toward the smoky interior of his father's club. Voices raised, shouting in German and French, about country, patriotism, and the emptiness of the German soul.

Then finally the shot, silencing everyone, including the piano player, who had been playing American boogie-woogie as if it could cover the ugliness in the room.

The smoke seemed to clear. Solae's father stood for the longest time, before collapsing in on himself. The Germans kicked him to see if he was still alive, and when he did not move, they stood. In a loud voice, the German who shot Solae's father ordered the piano player to play "Ein Prosit," and this time, the piano player did.

Solae had hurried through the crowd to retrieve his father's body. His mother did the same, running from her position behind the wings.

But they both arrived too late. His father vanished into the floor boards, his soul stolen by the stone he landed on, his essence gone as if it had never been.

Solae's mother had not been the same since. Solae had taken her and his brother away from that place, which the piano player took over and allowed to become a Vichy stronghold. Solae only hoped that the French who collaborated with the Boche were being haunted by the vengeful ghost of his father, and were suffering hideous torment because of it.

That was early in the Occupation, before the Germans began to understand Paris. The so-called decadence of Paris—the homosexuals, the mixed race couples, the transvestites who performed at the very best clubs, not to mention the Jews who corrupted (in the opinion of the Boche) every city they touched—disgusted and fascinated the German soldiers and bureaucrats who had invaded the city.

When the Boche discovered that Paris was a haven for yet another group—a group the Germans had slaughtered centuries ago—they were merciless. Faerie were murdered on the street, and no one came to their defense. For faerie were not French nor were they even human. They were something Other, and as food became scarce, they became little more than mongrel dogs to those who competed with them for every scrap.

Still, faerie were reluctant to leave Paris. They could not go to England, where they had been slaughtered centuries before the Germans came after them, and they could not afford the long trips to America—back in the days before the Americans became part of the war.

The countryside held the same dangers as the city, more so because there were fewer faerie and more Boche, and parts of France had become more German than others.

Faerie finally found themselves relegated to the land no one else wanted, the place no one else would think of as a refuge: the vast tombs beneath the city—the catacombs.

***

THAT WAS WHERE SOLAE slipped now. He went onto the side street through a small, private doorway that faerie kept locked. The Boche thought the doorway led to the courtyard for the apartments above, and never investigate.

Although the doorway did lead to a courtyard, beyond the courtyard was a street, a tiny street that the Boche car would never fit on. Part of the ancient city, the street meandered for less than a mile before reaching another boulevard through another doorway.

But underneath the street ran a main section of the catacombs. Solae had discovered the entrance one afternoon when he had explored. Then he had shown it to the elders, and they had used their combined powers to mask the entrance as a whitewashed wall.

Solae touched that wall now. His fingers found the latch that released the stone door, and it swung open, echoing in the emptiness.

He hated the catacombs. They were dark and dank, and they reeked of death. The Real Ones could not smell it, although they did not care for the catacombs either. But the Real Ones had lost their sense of the Beyond, and they did not realize that when their ancestors emptied Paris's graveyards and stacked the bones in the sewers beneath the city, they had stacked the power of death there as well.

Each time Solae descended into the darkness, he felt like he lost a part of himself. He had become convinced that his thinness was not due to his lack of meals, but to the pieces of himself taken by the darkness that lived below.

Still, he disappeared behind the stone door. As it closed behind him, he raised his right hand, pressed his thumb and forefinger together, and created a light.

The ability to create light was his only awe-inspiring power. A worthless power, his father used to say. But Solae did not think it worthless any longer, and he often wished that his father still lived so that Solae could prove how valuable the light had become.

Solae held his hand out before him. The light he formed was small—he didn't want to burn himself out this early in the day—and shaped like a flame. Only it did not flicker. The light burned steadily like an electric current, providing constant illumination for his journey ahead.

That was the only way he could tolerate heading into the catacombs. Flickering light would have terrified him, caused him to see ghosts in the shadows where there were none.

The Boche had come below many times, but had found no one. Only rats. For the Boche, for all of their posturing, were the most superstitious race in Europe—and the most terrified of death. They avoided the catacombs as much as possible.

The steps leading down had been carved centuries before by unknown hands, and hollowed by thousands of feet. In the time that Solae had spent below, he wondered at who moved the bones of the ancient dead. What kind of man would carry skeletons from their natural resting places to the depths below?

The bones were not just placed in a pile. They were stacked neatly in patterns, and the patterns shifted. In some places, the skulls formed a congregation of a thousand empty eyes, staring into the passageway. In others, the skulls were the center of a skull and cross bones motif.

Solae had found other places where the long bones of the legs and arms formed crosses or stars or other patterns that had existed since the beginning of time. In the middle of one particularly dark night, he had even found a group of bones that formed swastikas—and he had to remind himself that the symbol had been around long before the Boche took it for their own.

The catacombs were deep underground, and he always knew he drew close when water from the ceiling began to fall like rain. He worried that one day, the roof would collapse under the weight of the water above, but others, older and wiser than he, swore that would not happen.

Still, in many places below, the stone floor was wet, and the ceiling even wetter. He had to go through such a place to find his family, huddled in their little sepulchre deep within the labyrinth.

At first, Solae's mother had balked at staying in such a place. Clearly the priests who had designed this place had set up many areas for worship. There were long communion tables with all of the Christian symbols carved into the sides. There were quotes carved from the Real One's Holy Book upon the ceiling. There was an altar in the center, and even a baptismal font filled that collected ceiling rain.

Solae had to sleep on the communion table one night alone before his mother believed that one of these abandoned churches would be safe for faerie. And even now, she still had her doubts, occasionally waking in the middle of the night screaming that the crossbones on the wall were coming for her, to put her down like the dog the Christians believed she was.

She was nothing like the woman who bore him, nothing like the glamorous creature who performed every midnight on his father's stage. Then her alto voice had mesmerized the crowd, and her dark eyes had shown with magic unused. She had become the toast of their arrondisement, the center of faerie life in Paris—and beloved among the Real Ones themselves.

Or so it seemed.

When she had gone to the Real Ones after Solae's father's death, they had slammed their doors as if they did not know her. Solae's brother Noene suggested this was because they had not recognized her; to them she was a musical beauty in a smoke-filled room, not a woman with haunted eyes who needed refuge.

Solae brought the bread, only to find his mother sitting on the priest's chair, carved in marble and pushed against the stone wall—the only wall without bones protruding from it.

Noene was there with a sausage he had stolen, and together they made a feast. The three of them hadn't eaten that well in days.

After they finished, his mother looked at Solae. For a moment, he thought she would ask him how he had gotten the bread—how he had survived in the city above.

But she hadn't ever asked him about that. In fact, she did not speak of the city, as if it had ceased to exist. She hadn't been above ground for four years. It had affected not just her manner, but her sight. Solae had to douse his personal light, and find candles for the lamps below. She preferred the gloom, claiming that anything brighter made her eyes hurt.

"They've returned," his mother said.

Solae started. The Boche had come into this sanctuary more than once. The last time, Solae had been asleep on the communion table when he heard the clatter of boots against stone. He had doused the candles and climbed into the space between the skulls and the ceiling—a space barely a foot in width.

He had lain there, his nose pressed against the damp, the bones of the dead digging into his back, as the Boche peered into the chamber.

I cannot believe someone would hide here, one of them said in their hideous tongue. I would die first.

And then they had moved on, boots clanking with military precision, the click-clicks marking the time it took the Boche to leave Solae behind.

"Where did you hide?" Solae asked, hoping that his frail mother did not have to lie on bones as he had.

"Not the Germans," Noene said. "The Communists."

Solae suppressed his sigh of relief. The Communists were French, and they were not as frightening as his family made them sound. The Communists were part of the Resistance, the French who opposed the collaborationists who had taken the center of French government from Paris and moved it to Vichy to hide the fact that the Germans really controlled all that they did.

Vichy had become a dirtier word than Communist, and collaborationist the dirtiest word of all.

"You heard them?" Solae asked, pretending a concern he did not feel.

"They are plotting violence," his mother said, as if the violence she spoke of was directed at her.

"They say the Americans have landed in Normandy." Noene could not hide his enthusiasm. "They worry that De Gaulle will come here and destroy them."

That was not the real worry of the Communists. Solae knew more about them than he told his family. He had found the Communist enclave long ago, and during the dark nights, had snuck through the bones to find the enclave, listening to the speeches and the pep talks and the news.

It was from them that Solae had picked up the word "Boche" which suited the Germans much more than any other word had. He did not want to speak of them with respect. He needed a word that was profane for what they had done to his city, his family, his home.

The Communists had taken to hiding in the sewers more than the catacombs, and planning small attacks against Germans. They disarmed the Vichy police, they occasionally killed a stormtrooper who did found himself alone, and they sabotaged shipments of French goods back to Germany.

The Communists were only a small part of the Resistance, but they were hated by their own people, and feared, for when the Germans were defeated and Vichy gone, the Free French believed the Communists would rise up and take over the government—obligating the French to Stalin and the Soviet Union the way Vichy obligated France to Hitler.

But Solae did not share that fear. The Communists called themselves freedom fighters, and they were fierce advocates for France.

He admired all they did. Sometimes he sat in the shadows and listened as they made their plans. He wished he could help them, but he could not. If someone died—even accidentally—because of his involvement, he would lose what little magic he had.

For that was why faerie were so easily defeated throughout Europe. Their powers were the powers of life, lost when touched with death. Faerie resisted coming into the catacombs for that very reason—even ancient death disturbed them.

It took a courageous few to live below, test their powers, and report the others before the entire community found the shelter and safety they needed.

Solae wished he could help the Communists. He did what he could. He was what some called a passive member of the Resistance—he taunted the Boche, stole from them or their Vichy compatriots, and destroyed their writings wherever he found them. Sometimes he siphoned precious gas from their cars, but carefully, never allowing his powers of light to touch the liquid for fear of a fire.

He did what he could, but it was very little.

"Aren't you worried by this?" Noene asked. "They will start a war above us."

"There is a war above us," Solae said.

"But not like the countryside," Noene said. "Paris still stands."

For the moment. But Solae did not say that. Instead, he said, "They say De Gaulle will be here by the first of September and I believe it. Many of the Germans who are not soldiers have stolen what they can from the city and fled."

"What will happen to us?" his mother asked. "If Communists find us, they are even more ruthless than the Germans."

She was thinking of the Russian communists. She had lost family in St. Petersburg, which the communists had then renamed. Sometimes, she said lately, her entire life had been about loss.

"We'll be fine," Solae said. But he did not believe that, for the Germans were ruthless. He had seen too much to believe they would let Paris go so easily.

His thoughts made him restless. He stood, unable to stay in the darkness much longer.

"It's still daylight above," he said. "I'll see if I can find us anything else before night falls."

He did not wait for his mother's answer. Instead, he fled through the tunnels, and went up to the light.

***

HE HEARD THE SOUND before he even left the stairway—gunfire. The heat had grown worse, a physical presence that made the gunfire seem even more ominous. As he stepped through the doorway, this one leading to a different part of the city, he saw German tanks in the street.

Four of them, large as houses. The tanks made Solae shudder. He pressed himself against the wall, uncertain what to do. He did not know if he had been seen, if his presence would lead others to the catacombs.

The gunfire came from the Hôtel de Ville, the city hall. Men—boys, really—leaned out of windows and shot at the tanks with revolvers.

The tanks swiveled, aiming their guns at the Hôtel de Ville. The building itself seemed to shudder from their might. Solae winced, feeling helpless.

He had heard that the Germans would destroy the city before they allowed the French to retake it, but he had not believed it. Paris was, according the BBC, the only intact city left in Europe. It had artifacts and treasures that everyone—not just the French—could enjoy.

It was his home.

A young woman, standing near his hiding place, screamed at the Boche. Solae couldn't make out the words—something about leaving her city in peace—then she grabbed a bottle from the ground beside her, and ran for the street.

His heart pounded. He stepped forward to stop her—there was nothing she could do against tanks—but she kept screaming, "Filthy Boche! You do not belong here! Filthy Boche!"

Solae could not reach her.

She got to the side of the tank, smashed her bottle against its open turret, and somehow flames exploded along the metal. Solae had heard about such weapons—simple combinations of chemicals that he did not understand.

He heard a scream from inside, saw a German soldier rise, slapping himself, trying to put out the fire his clothing had become.

The girl grinned and ran back toward Solae, her steps almost a dance. For a moment, he remembered the beauty his father conferred upon the non-beautiful—a touch of glamour, given by a little bit of magic.

The girl had that magic, without Solae's father's help. She was not faerie, and yet she glowed with her victory.

Her gaze met Solae's and he thought he had never seen anything so lovely in his entire life.

And then a shot rang out.

A single shot, even though he knew it could not have been the only one, even though he knew others were firing.

But it was as if he were with the girl, as if he were linked to her by her moment of victory. He saw the surprise fill her eyes, the blood spatter out of her mouth, her look of triumph turn to horror—

And then to nothing.

She stumbled, collapsed, and fell forward, like his father had done. Like so many others had done.

Solae did not stop to think. He ran into the street, to the girl, as people around him shouted, demanding that he take cover. The tanks kept shelling the Hôtel de Ville and, in one heart-stopping moment, he feared the building would tumble around him.

He reached her and crouched, knowing from her open and glazed eyes that she was gone. But he could not leave her there. Even if the stone would not absorb her soul the way it had absorbed his father's, Solae could not abandon her on the street, to be run over by the Boche, to be treated as one more rag in a city littered with them.

He slipped his hands under her arms and lifted her. Bullets pinged off the cobblestones as someone shot at him—maybe even the freedom fighters above, missing their German targets.

His heart was pounding, the girl's blood warm on his skin. She had had her moment against the Boche, her victory, and the Boche had stolen it from her, as they had stolen everything else—her home, her life, her world.

Solae's world.

He carried her to the sidewalk, where one of the old women wailed in grief. Then he set the girl's body, and knew what he had to do.

The Boche were the most superstitious creatures in Europe.

Solae turned to face them.

The boys still fired from the windows above. Three of the tanks still fired at the Hôtel de Ville. The fourth, its crew disabled or dead thanks to the girl, huddled like a wounded animal in the middle of the street.

Solae formed a fist and held it high, in mockery of the German salute.

"*Achtung!*" he shouted, his German flawless from years of listening to the vile tongue.

No one looked at him. No one seemed to see him.

He used his own glamour, his ability to brighten a room.

"*Achtung!*" he shouted again, and this time, every German within hearing range looked.

Solae squinted slightly, concentrating. He imagined his entire fist engulfed in flame—and suddenly it was. Cool flame which did not consume, but which burned beautifully in the bright August sunlight.

The shooting from the windows stopped.

He let the fire slide down his arm and engulf his entire body. The street looked wavy through the flame, as if he were viewing everything from a heat mirage.

"*Vive le France!*" he shouted.

Then he made the fire wink out.

The Germans stared at him for the longest time. The moment seemed to stretch forever.

Solae smiled at them.

"*Vive le France!*" he repeated, and put his hands on his hips, obviously unharmed by the fire that had surrounded him a moment before.

He took a step forward, and the German closest to him screamed. So did another, and another. They scrambled into their tanks, down the turrets, closing the hatches.

Solae remained on the street, watching them. The Germans drove their tanks away from him, their terror palpable in the thick August heat.

Dust rose around him. He did not feel the girl's sense of victory. All he had done was a trick, nothing monumental, nothing worth a life.

But the boys in the windows above started to cheer. And so did the people on the street. They were looking at him, and cheering, and he could not take it.

He had done nothing. He was nothing. Just a small man with a small talent, and a little bit of luck.

He could not save the girl from death. He could not prevent death. And he had used his one talent the only way he knew how.

The cheering continued, and he looked away. The girl's corpse remained on the sidewalk, the old woman bent over her, rocking, as if the movement would make the girl return.

Nothing would make her return. Nor would Solae's father return, or their life, or his mother's sanity. Nothing would be the same again, no matter when the Allies came.

All these years, he had deluded himself, hiding among the dead, believing that all he had to do was wait, and life would return to normal. The humans would stop their craziness, the war would fade, and everything would return.

But it was not just a human craziness. His father had been right: there were humans to ally with, and humans to fight. His father would have fought—he had fought, in his own turf, over his own command: music.

But Solae had not. He had not used his powers at all.

Until now.

All these years, he could have fought in a slightly larger way, and he had not.

He had not.

While others died.

He had chosen to fade away instead of bringing light. He had chosen to live among the dead instead of fight beside the living.

But he would not make that choice again.

He could bring light to darkness, and vanish seemingly without a trace.

The Resistance was chasing the Boche from Paris, and Solae would help as best he could. And when he was done here, he would help liberate all of France, which was the world he cared about.

He finally knew how to do it, without losing his powers, without betraying his people.

He would haunt the Boche. He would bring light to the darkest corners of their souls, exposing them to all they had done.

He would destroy the Boche, taking all they feared and turning it against them, one by one.

One superstitious mind at a time.

Subtle Interpretations

*L*IEUTENANT RICHARD COOPER found her in the Paris International Telephone Exchange. She sat in the large hot room, her black hair pulled into a bun, and legs crossed at the ankle and off to the side like the photographic models he'd met. She leaned forward as she spoke into the microphone, plugging metal edged prongs into lit areas of the electronic board.

The room was a cacophony of women's voices, something he hadn't heard for years, that high-pitched, warm sound of dozens of women speaking all at once. It didn't matter that they spoke mostly in French; what mattered was the musicality and softness of their voices, the way that they all put a hand to the headphones as if adjusting an earring.

He had come to interview the best among them, the ones who could handle most international calls as the call came in, switching from French to Russian to English without a breath, helping the unseen caller on the other end get connected with the correct exchange or the right person.

He watched from the supervisor's booth, just above the main doors. Even the window looking down was hot. Fans worked the back and on the ceiling. The rooms below had no ventilation, but they were where the equipment still was, in a basement, protecting everything from bombs that never came.

Most of the women below were matronly, and those that weren't looked hard, as if nothing could surprise them. Their clothing, which ten years before would have been fashionable, was worn and thin, their shoes so old that they looked scuffed even from a distance.

"Let's see how good they are," he said to Yves LeRoi, the man who ran this part of the exchange. "All except that one."

He pointed at the woman he'd been staring at. She sat in the exact center, and unlike the other women, she did not look tired. Her touch on the headset was light, her movements economical. She might have been a touch too thin, but her face hadn't hardened into a mask of suppressed hate.

"Mademoiselle Renard?" he asked. "But she is the best. I believed you would want her. She is fluent in six languages that I know of, and perhaps more."

Cooper sighed. His boss, Lieutenant Commander Alfred Steer, had told him repeatedly that finding the best translator was imperative. All other considerations had to be set aside, even if he felt the woman was too beautiful to live among GIs for several months.

"All right then," he said. "I'll listen to her as well."

***

COOPER, STEER, AND A HANDFUL of deputies had only a few weeks to find the best translators in Europe. And not just translators who worked well on paper, but translators who could handle simultaneous translation from one language into another.

They were conducting an experiment on the world's largest stage, the International Military Tribunal at Nuremberg. The man in charge of setting up the tribunal, Judge Robert Jackson, had somehow gotten IBM to speed up production on its experimental simultaneous-translation equipment. The equipment would be tested—in action—at the trial of high-level Germans for war crimes.

Although many were disappointed that Hitler wasn't on the dock—the coward had killed himself as Allied troops entered Berlin—many of his henchmen were. From Hermann Göring, Hitler's number two man, to Field Marshall Wilhelm Keitel, the chief of staff of the German Armed Forces, every surviving Nazi leader would sit in that courtroom and answer for his crimes.

And in order for this trial to work, the judges, from all the Allied countries, would have to hear translations in their own language, while the defendants would have to hear the same words in German. Cooper was told to be prepared for every possible European language, just in case the witnesses spoke something other than French, German, English, Russian or Italian.

The task, when Steer explained it, seemed impossible. Particularly with only a few weeks to find the right candidates. Especially after the debacle at the League of Nations in Geneva. Steer and Cooper had gone there themselves, expecting to find the best translators in all of Europe.

Instead, they found dusty old men who hadn't lifted their heads out of texts in decades. One of the reasons the League failed, in Cooper's opinion, was that everyone had to present a position paper, wait until it was translated, and then conduct questions and answers on the page so that the translators would have time to find the exact right word.

As Jackson had told them before they left, Steer and Cooper didn't have time to find the right word. But they had to find the best verbal translators. Because if the translations were even slightly incorrect, the trial would fail. The defendants could claim that they had not heard the same evidence as everyone else.

Before he sent them to Nuremberg, he would see if they had the basic skills to translate on the fly. Once in the city, they'd be tested for accuracy and speed. He just had to find the most able linguists in all of Europe.

He had been given this assignment because his German was good, but his French was excellent. He understood a small amount of Italian, and had gained enough Russian to make casual conversation. He knew a smattering of other languages.

But he had failed one of the early translation tests. His mind froze—literally froze—when he had to speak in one language while listening to another.

He knew how hard this task would be. He also knew that a war crimes trial would include testimony he did not want his mother or his sister to hear. And then there was the problem of Nuremberg itself, a ruined city filled with starving people, too many lonely GIs, and not enough women.

That was why he didn't want the young beauty to join the team. He would discourage her if he could.

His early interviews went well. LeRoi had shown him to a small room, several floors above the international exchange. Someone had brought a carafe of American coffee and a single cup for him. A nearby table held an assortment of cheeses and baked goods.

He made use of all the refreshments during the interviews.

The interviews happened individually. So he had time to ask each woman to sit, and make herself comfortable, tell him about herself. After three interviews, he also started with a speech, telling the women he didn't care how they spent the war. He was tired of hearing made-up tales of being in the Resistance. If every French woman had been in the Resistance, France would not have surrendered. The country would have been able to fight, no matter what the politicians did.

A lot of the women had lost their husbands or sons, and wanted out of Paris. Most hadn't been able to leave before the city surrendered because they lacked the money. They had some now, but they had no idea where to go. The entire world was different and they no longer knew where they belonged.

Some of the best candidates turned him down instantly when they heard that they had to go to Germany. (*I have had enough of the Boche,* they'd say. *I do not care what kind of wages you pay.*)

But others lit up when they heard they'd make double, sometimes triple what they were making now. Their food would be provided and so would their accommodations. For many of these women, the job he offered seemed like the answer to their prayers.

He had a hard time explaining that they'd be tested in Nuremberg and sent home if they couldn't perform the task to Leon Dostert's specifications. Dostert was the man in charge of this program. He was an Army colonel who had been one of Eisenhower's chief interpreters during the war. That was the unusual part of this program. People from all branches of the military had come together, brought for their talents instead of following some personnel quota.

Colonel Dostert was trying to convince Cooper to reup, just to have him on hand in case the translation program failed. Cooper couldn't imagine himself whispering in the ear of some French journalist, and had delayed making a decision until this task was done.

Part of his brain played with the notion as he listened to the women's enthusiasm. He understood the ones who said no. But the ones who said yes suddenly looked younger, as if he had given them hope.

He had just gotten up to get a brioche and pour himself more coffee when she came in. LeRoi had called her Mademoiselle Renard.

Cooper set the brioche back on the tray and went to his notes. Her first name was Nathalie, which did not suit her. He would have given her a more exotic name, something that sounded a lot more foreign.

She did not smile when she saw him. Instead, she nodded just once and waited for him to offer her a seat. Then she slipped into the chair, folding her legs to one side as she had done in the exchange.

"I'm Robert Cooper," he said, deciding to leave off his rank. His uniform made his position clear. He was an American, and he was in the military. She didn't need to know more. "I am with the International Military Court in Nuremberg. Have you heard of it?"

"I have been following the news," she said stiffly. He wondered for a moment if French was her native language. But her name suggested that it was.

He did not have complete dossiers on any of the women. They would provide as much information as they could, but on some levels, he would just have to trust.

"We are in need of translators," he said, settling into his speech. He picked up his pen, pulled the paper with her name on it aside, and made a line, as he had done with all the others. "What languages do you speak fluently?"

"I do not know," she said. "Many."

He had never had that answer before. He frowned at her. She had folded her hands across her shabby dress. She was smaller than she had looked from above, her features delicate. Her eyebrows, plucked to a thin line, swept upward, and she had clearly replenished her makeup before coming into the room.

"How many?" he asked.

"I do not know," she said again. "I have a gift."

He wanted to roll his eyes. All interpreters had a gift for language or they would not be able to do their job. "Give me a guess."

She shrugged one shoulder. "Ten? Twenty? I am not sure."

Either she didn't understand him or he was asking the wrong question. He switched to German. "Tell me which languages you speak fluently."

"I do not know," she said in that language.

"The key word," he said in English, "is 'fluently.' I need translators who know all sorts of idioms, and have large vocabularies."

"I love words," she said in American English, the accent Midwestern and strong. "I remember every one I have heard."

"Then why is your speech so formal?" he asked in French.

"Because," she said in the same language, "this is an interview. Would you like me to be less formal?"

"Yes," he said in Russian. "Tell me your name."

"Technically," she said in that language, "you just told me to 'give' you my name. It is an American construction, not a Russian one."

"Your name," he said in Polish.

"Nathalie," she said in Polish, after a slight pause. Her pronunciation of her own name did not have the soft "th" that the French version had. It had a harder "t," just like it should. "It is on that paper before you."

He didn't have any more languages to test her with. But he wasn't supposed to test. He was supposed to get simple answers to simple questions.

He decided to move on. He asked in English, "Where were you born?"

"Paris," she said.

"Here, then," he said in French.

"I've never been to Paris, Texas," she said in American English. The accent was Texan this time. "I believe it's the only other Paris on the map, but I could be wrong."

The hair rose on the back of his neck. Her accents—at least for American English—were uncanny. He had never heard anything like it.

"You can mimic," he said in English. "What other accents can you do?"

"In English?" she asked.

"Sure," he said.

"I do prefer the British upper class," she said with a posh accent. "Bu' coc'ney suits me just fine, guv'nor."

His breath caught. "And in French?"

"Well, everyone knows there is Parisian French," she said in French, using a refined Paris accent. "But most non-natives do not realize that French has many different accents as well. And variations. Would you like to hear Canadian, which many of my people say is not French? Or Cajun, which is old bastardized French or perhaps—"

"Enough." He was unnerved.

She leaned back in her chair, subdued. As she spoke of the languages and accents, she had seemed animated for the first time. Her eyes had sparkled, and what he had initially thought was rouge was actually a natural red that wisped across her high cheekbones.

"I did not mean to scare you," she said, in that same formal French she had started with. "For this reason, I do not tell people of my gift."

"Monsieur LeRoi says you are his most talented operator."

"He believes I have learned phrases in various languages. I have not disabused him."

Cooper set down his pen and templed his fingers, banging the tips against his chin. "Why are you telling me, then?"

"Because I am tired of saying *Buena Sierra! Guten Tag! Es posible a ayudarle?* I would like important work."

"Helping people place calls is not important?" Cooper asked.

"Not like during the war. Then I thought each call might be, as you say in English, life or death." She switched from French to English with the word "English."

"Have you family here?" he asked.

"Not any more." Her voice was soft. One woman before her had burst into tears when he asked that question.

"What other jobs have you had?" he asked.

"This," she said. "I started for Monsieur LeRoi when I was eighteen. I told him I had a gift. He did not care. He needed women to risk their lives in a place that might become a target if the Allies had decided to bomb France."

He had heard this before as well—communications were always vulnerable to the bombings—but he also knew that no one had targeted Paris, nor did anyone want to. Venice had been the same way, a pristine island in a sea of rubble.

"How old are you now?" he asked.

"I will be twenty-five in December," she said.

He had the odd sense that she was lying. But she had at least told him her age. So many of the other French women hadn't, slipping instead into that coy flirtatiousness that was a little too sexual for his hick American tastes.

"They tell us the trial will end in December," he said. "But I don't believe it. I think it could take a long time. My boss says that translators must prepare to be gone for six months, minimum. Would that be hard for you?"

She shook her head.

"On the other hand," he said, "we might send you back after two weeks. We have to test your skills, you see. We—"

"Is that not what you just did?" she asked.

"No," he said. "You'll be tested in your ability to speak one language while…"

He went through the speech again. It was as if he were a record stuck in a groove. He could probably say that speech in his sleep, in both English and French. Maybe he should try it in German once or twice, just to mix things up.

When he finished, he said, "Does that sound like something you want to try?"

She nodded.

"Then you have to tell me which languages you would like to be tested in."

"Whichever ones you need," she said.

He sighed. "I have to write something down. Preferably the names of the languages. We'll start with French."

She smiled and watched as he wrote *French* and *English*.

"If you want to try other languages, tell Colonel Dostert in Nuremberg when you show up for the test, okay?"

"Okay," she said, and this time, he heard his own Midwestern roots in her voice.

"Let me tell you the pay schedule, and then ask a few more questions." He tapped the pen against the page. "And I have to say, if I feel like you're toying with me, I won't send you to Nuremberg."

"I am not a cat," she said. "I do not toy with anything."

***

YET BY THE END of the interview, he wondered. He still had that odd sense that she was lying to him. After she left, he sent for LeRoi.

"Do you have any papers for her?" Cooper asked. "Some kind of file?"

"I have her work records. Hours, pay records, that sort of thing." LeRoi sat in the chair the women had sat in. He looked smaller than they had, and older, as if the war had diminished him.

"What about a resume? Some kind of application? Any personal history?"

LeRoi smiled. The smile was slow and knowing. "You are interested in her."

Cooper was, much as he didn't want to be. He took non-fraternization rules seriously. Or he had, until he saw her.

"For our project, yes. But she's not being forthcoming. I need to know how many languages she speaks, how old she really is, and where she comes from."

"I do not have such papers," LeRoi said. "I have not found a language she cannot speak. I send for her if someone is having trouble, and within a moment, she can resolve the problem. She is truly gifted."

"That's what she said." Cooper tapped his pen on the page. "If you don't have any background on her, how did you come to hire her?"

"I had a sign, asking for multilingual employees. She came in and dazzled me."

"By talking in half a dozen languages," Cooper said dryly.

"I could not find one she did not know. I even sent for one of our older employees. He had been a missionary in China and spoke some of that language."

The Chinese spoke many languages, but Cooper did not correct LeRoi.

"She was able to answer him. Then they had a discussion, until his Chinese wore out, not hers. I hired her on the spot."

Interesting. Cooper kept tapping his pen. He was so used to the Navy. All the regulations and approvals had become part of his life. And he was becoming more and more paranoid. He wanted everyone checked out. After being in

Germany for two months, he found himself believing that everyone could be a spy. Even though the German government—Hitler's government—was gone, there were the Russians. Even though they were allies, he hated them, every one he'd met, with a passion that surprised him.

"What do you know about her then?" Cooper asked. "The personal things."

LeRoi smiled that odd smile again. "She lives near the Sorbonne. She lives alone, so far as I can tell, and never speaks of family. Nor do young men come for her, and she does not participate in those discussions about husbands lost at the front. For all her languages, she says little to the other women here. She keeps to herself."

"What happened to her family?" Cooper asked.

LeRoi shrugged. "What has happened to most, I suppose. Even for France, it has been a difficult few years."

Cooper didn't reply to that. Paris stood. The French countryside was lovely. Families escaped or they survived under the Vichy regime. A few got caught resisting. Some became sport for the Nazis.

And, he supposed, hundreds—maybe thousands—of French Jews were sent to the camps. He did not know and he did not ask.

He tried not to talk about the camps. He had been to Bergen Belsen just before going to Nuremberg, trying to get statements from the survivors.

He doubted he would ever speak of the camps again.

"*Monsieur*?" LeRoi leaned forward.

Apparently Cooper had been silent longer than he thought. "I am supposed to take the best candidates with me. Do you know any reason why she shouldn't go into Germany?"

"No one should go to Germany," LeRoi said. "It should rot. But beside that? She is my best employee. If you do not want her, I shall gladly keep her. She is a gem."

"She is, isn't she?" Cooper said. "She truly is."

***

THE GEM STOOD outside the Telephone Exchange as he left. She was smoking a cigarette and looking down the street for the bus. He looked too. It was only a few blocks away.

"Have you had dinner?" he asked.

She whirled, as if she hadn't realized he was there. Then she blinked, and he thought for a moment that she didn't understand him.

That would be impossible, though, right? Maybe she hadn't heard him.

"Dinner?" she repeated, just as he was about to ask again.

"Yes." He regretted the invitation now. He hadn't asked any of the other women.

It was just another sign that he was tired, tired of the rules, tired of not having a normal life.

She smiled. Her entire face transformed. She was, without a doubt, the most beautiful woman he had ever seen.

"I would love to," she said. She pinched out her cigarette, then carefully set it in a small metal cigarette case that she kept in her purse.

Suddenly he wasn't sure if she was coming to dinner because she wanted to be with him or because she hadn't had a decent meal in months.

It probably didn't matter. He shouldn't have asked in the first place.

He took her arm and together they walked down the street to a small restaurant that had somehow survived all the deprivations. He had loved this restaurant before the war, and had been pleased that it was still here.

She stopped at the door.

"It's all right," he said. "I know it's expensive, but the meal is courtesy of the American government."

She shook her head. "That's not it. This was a Boche favorite. I...I cannot get past the sense that it is somehow tainted."

"Is there someplace else?" he asked. "I'd be happy to learn of a new restaurant."

She straightened her shoulders as if that made her stronger. "All of the good ones, they are Boche favorites. I must get past this."

Then she pushed open the door and stepped inside.

After the remains of daylight on the street, the interior seemed dark. As he followed her down the stairs that led to the dining room, he too felt a bit of unease.

He blamed it on his actions—his request for this date—because he didn't want to believe the Germans could have tainted everything like she said. If that were the case, nothing that survived had any value at all.

A maitre d', stiffly formal in his tuxedo, led them to a table in the back. The table was around a corner, and like most in this place, was very private.

He handed them the menus, advised Cooper on wines as if he were the most ignorant man on the planet, and Cooper smiled because he couldn't help himself. Before the war, the French had treated Americans like bumpkins, but after the liberation, Americans had become gods. He was happy to return to bumpkin status. It meant, in some places at least, things were returning to normal.

Nathalie stroked the linen tablecloth as if it were made of gold. Then she fingered the crystal water glass.

"We can still go somewhere else," Cooper said.

"No." She picked up the glass and took a sip. "It is nice to know such things survived. So much did not."

"Your family?" He hadn't meant to ask the question so crudely, and yet he had, proving that he was an American bumpkin.

She nodded her head once. "My family."

"Were they in Paris?"

She raised her chin. "Until the trains took them."

"You're Jewish?" He couldn't quite rid his voice of the surprise he felt. She didn't look Jewish. And then he cursed that thought. It was the kind of thought that led to the walking skeletons that he had seen—the very idea that someone's religion could be seen just by the shape of their face. Sometimes, he felt, he was no better than the men he had defeated.

"Would it matter?" she asked, apparently catching his tone.

"Not to me," he said. "But the Tribunal might be hard for you. The war crimes these men are accused of include what happened to people who boarded those trains."

All the beauty leached from her face. What remained was a hatred so deep he nearly slid his chair backwards.

"I am aware of that," she said.

"Can you faithfully translate what's said? No embellishments, no changes?"

"Of course." Her tone was flat as well. He wondered if he was hearing her real accent for the first time.

"What about testimony about the camps? I've been there. I've taken some. It's—"

He stopped, and waved a hand in lieu of finishing, as his stomach turned.

"I am not delicate," she said.

"I know," he said. "I'm not either. But this…"

She shrugged. "Humans have always been brutal, no?"

A waiter arrived with their wine. The rituals—opening the bottle, sniffing the cork, taking a sip—prevented Cooper from answering. He wasn't sure he had an answer anyway.

"I can do your job," she said as the waiter left. "In fact, you want me."

He did want her. He touched her hand lightly. Her skin was smooth and warm. She glanced at him as if his fingertips had given her a small shock.

He certainly felt that way.

"This job will be hard," he said. "I don't want it to harm you."

Her smile was bitter. "I have already been harmed. At worst, I shall be reminded on a daily basis. As you Americans say, so what? So many others no longer have days. It is better to live and to be aware of the living, is it not, than to hide as if the past has never happened?"

He wasn't sure. But for this moment, he was willing to go with the thought, to believe what she said.

As the waiter returned, this time with menus, Cooper steered the conversation away from the job and the war, finding, to his surprise, that she loved music as much as he did—all kinds ("particularly," she said, "your American jazz"), and that she was wider read than he could ever imagine being.

He had never met a woman with such breadth of knowledge, particularly on the things that interested him, and it fascinated him.

She fascinated him.

They talked for hours, and then he walked her home. The student district, once the site of protests and unusual political attitudes, seemed subdued and quiet. The narrow cobblestone streets still had smoke-stains from the fighting that occurred here between the Resistance and the Germans as news of the Allied approach reached Paris.

She lived on a charming side street, the walls of the buildings laced with flowering vines. Elaborate ironwork covered the doors. She stopped in front of one, whose ironwork imitated the creeping vines nearby.

He started to take her hand, about to give her a friendly American handshake, when she raised her head to his. Her mouth was small and perfect, her cheeks still flushed, her eyes so dark they seemed infinite. Before he could stop himself, he dipped his head.

She lifted her chin ever so slightly, and their lips brushed. Then he pulled her to him, and kissed her. She slipped her arms around his back, holding him against her, and deepened the kiss. He felt dizzy and aroused at the same time, barely able to contain himself.

"Upstairs?" she whispered, but he wasn't sure which language she used.

"Yes," he answered in English, and they could barely stop kissing long enough for her to fumble with the lock. He half-carried her up a flight of stairs, and then another. She giggled against his mouth when he tripped, catching himself on the plaster walls.

"One more," she whispered, and he hoped she was referring to the flights of stairs, not to the kisses.

She pulled him up the last flight, then pushed open an old door, and led him inside an attic room, decorated with more flowering plants than he'd ever seen inside. They crowded the two windows, spilled over the tables and chairs, and nearly covered the floor.

She unfolded the couch into a bed, then grabbed him by his belt and yanked him onto the lumpy mattress.

And there, surrounded by the scent of her and flowers he couldn't name, he fell in love.

***

HE BARELY MADE IT to the seven a.m. check-in breakfast. He didn't have time to go back to his hotel room. His uniform was wrinkled, his hair still wet.

She hadn't had a shower, just one of those silly hand-held things he'd seen all over Europe. She'd had to help him turn it on, and her presence in the tiny bathroom had delayed him even more.

He had promised to find her for lunch. He would meet her just outside the Telephone Exchange. He already knew where he would take her.

The meeting went longer than he planned. It took place in the hotel's breakfast nook. When Cooper arrived, he got a knowing look from Steer. Cooper's own assistant, Andrew Gabler, raised his eyebrows in surprise. Gabler had gotten the fraternization lecture from Cooper. He felt his cheeks redden.

Cooper ate a soft-boiled egg and too many pastries as he told the other men about the women at the exchange. Then he handed his notes to Steer, who would give them to the head of the Paris unit to compare to known troublemakers.

Cooper's assignment this morning was, of all things, at the main Catholic diocese. Some of the priests, Gabler had learned, had linguistic abilities that extended beyond French, Latin, and ancient Greek. Cooper was to check that out.

The assignment embarrassed him almost as much as his appearance. Even though he wasn't Catholic, the last place he wanted to go to was a religious setting. He felt distinctly profane at the moment.

When breakfast finished, he hurried to his room, changed, and came back down. Gabler was waiting for him, that smile still on his face.

"Do I know her?" he asked.

Cooper shook his head.

"Do I want to?" Gabler's tone was suggestive.

Cooper felt a surge of anger, but pushed it back. He understood why Gabler had made that assumption. So many women all over Europe were poor, and many of them used the only thing they had left to make money.

"She's not like that," Cooper said.

"My," Gabler said. "*C'est l'amour*? So soon?"

"Shut up," Cooper said, and headed off to church.

***

ONE OF THE PRIESTS spoke excellent Greek. At least, Cooper thought it was excellent, but his Greek was terrible, so he needed help making the determination.

An hour before lunch, he stopped at headquarters to request his afternoon assignment and to get someone else to return to the diocese.

Cooper stepped inside military headquarters to the clatter of typewriters. Secretaries hurried back and forth, carrying messages and looking important. Men sat outside doors, hat in hand, waiting for meetings.

It almost seemed as if the war was still going on.

Matt Accordino, one of the general staff headquartered here, beckoned him forward. "I vetted your list."

Cooper took a seat beside Accordino's desk, almost in the aisle. A secretary, her skirt slit on the side against regulation, brushed against him as she passed.

"And?" Cooper asked.

"You have one questionable on here." Accordino pushed a file forward. "You have her as Nathalie Renard."

Cooper felt cold. "What's her real name?"

"Wish I could tell you. She went by half a dozen names. Renard is just one of them. It's actually one of the early ones. She must have gone back to it."

"What's the problem? Was she a collaborator?"

"Just the opposite," Accordino said. "She was with the Resistance."

Cooper let out a breath he hadn't realized he was holding. "Then what's the problem?"

"Her specialty." Accordino opened the file and tapped the top page. "High-level assassination."

***

COOPER WAS REELING as he headed to the Telephone Exchange. He'd glanced through the file. He really hadn't had time to read it all, even though it was one of the most complete dossiers he'd seen outside the German high command.

Of course, he realized halfway through looking at it, it was complete because much of it had been compiled by the Germans stationed in Paris. Nathalie Renard aka Marie Laurent aka Béatrice Brel murdered every single important German she had gotten close to. Calculated murders, all with different weapons, most usually done up close.

The Germans had no pictures of her, but the Americans found one when they arrived because she had dated an intelligence officer briefly in Brussels. Apparently she traveled all over the French-speaking world, trying to cozy up to Nazis, and assassinate them.

She succeeded more than she failed. She had moved up to high value targets by the end. The one she missed, the one she claimed to regret the most, was Göring. Her attempt on his life was the only failure she would admit to.

Göring. Who was now on trial in Nuremberg for crimes against humanity.

His death would not be a great loss. His death in custody of the Allies as he was about to go to trial would be an international scandal.

She was waiting outside the exchange, smoking the second half of that cigarette. When she saw him, she tossed the butt onto the sidewalk and ground it under her heel.

She did not smile. She seemed to sense immediately that something was wrong.

"Did it not go well?" she asked in very formal English.

"Well enough," he said.

"Are you in trouble for me?" It was the first linguistic mistake he'd heard from her. It surprised him, and made him wonder if she had sensed his nervousness.

"You mean for being with you?" he asked.

"Yes."

He leaned against a lamp post, his back to traffic coming up the road. Passersby would think he was flirting with her, and most likely avoid him. The post put him in an oddly vulnerable position, but he kept it, partly because he wanted to see her face, and partly because he didn't want to talk about this anywhere that they could be overhead.

"If I took you to Nuremberg," he said, his voice deliberately low. She had to lean in to hear him, "how long would it take you to murder Hermann Göring?"

She blanched, then turned her head. She fumbled in her purse for a moment, her hands shaking.

"What makes you think I would?"

The sentence didn't cover her, but it bought her time. He knew that, and was more surprised that she uttered it, that she stayed here, rather than taking off down the sidewalk.

"Heinrich Jessler, Joachim Mauser, and Otto van Kleghaurn."

She closed her eyes, then let out a small sigh.

"Or had you turned your attention to the Allies? Was I supposed to give you entry? Has someone hired you to disrupt the proceedings?"

Her eyes opened, as color rose on her cheeks. "You came to me. You solicited me. I have done nothing. I did not know who you were or what you wanted. I would never kill anyone who was not a Nazi. You know that. You have to know that."

Midway through that speech, she had switched to colloquial French and her accent became strongly Parisian. He was hearing her own accent for the first time. Her true voice.

And she was worried about what he thought. She was angry at him.

Could she be that good an actress? Or did she care about him too?

"But you weren't going to say no to the opportunity," he said. "If you could have murdered Göring, you would have."

"Your Tribunal will hang them, won't they?" She snapped her purse shut and pushed it up her arm to her elbow. "You wouldn't need me."

"We hang only the guilty ones."

"They're Boche," she said. "They're all guilty."

His heart was pounding hard. A few people passing on the street glanced at them, but no one stopped for long. If someone came to the bus stop, Cooper waved them on.

"So, in an international tribunal, with well-respected judges and jurists from all over the civilized world, you would act as judge, jury and executioner."

"I see the papers. You have your own executioner."

"Only if the prisoners are found guilty," Cooper said again.

"They will all be found guilty."

He shook his head. "This is not a show trial. They might not. We're stressing fairness. You know this."

"I do not believe it." She raised her chin. "I would have done you a good job."

"Killing the prisoners."

"Translating their words," she hissed.

"Tell me," he said. "How did you do it? Jessler and von Kleghaurn had guards standing only a few feet away from you. They saw no weapons."

Her skin was mottled. Tears lined her eyes. "Last night, you said we had something special. Last night, you said I was different than anyone else."

He nodded.

"How can you ask me?"

"I've asked you many things you haven't answered," he said. "Answer me this one."

She crossed her arms. "The Germans, they have killed my people since they found us. And then they made our stories theirs, so that the entire world would find us."

He shook his head. "What?"

"You asked if I was a Jew. I am not. Nor am I a Gypsy or any other race that is somehow unpure to those Nordic bastards. My people are older."

He didn't know of any people older than the Jews, but his knowledge of history was limited.

"I'm still not following."

"You've heard of us," she said. "You read the stories. The Grimm Brothers, no? You've read them in translation."

"You're a wicked stepmother?" he asked.

"*Merde*," she said. "You call it Faerie. You have heard of Faerie, have you not? My people are nearly gone. A few have hid, many have been deported and murdered, never fighting back, because we were raised that we would lose our magic if we fight."

She was now leaning so close to him that he could feel her breath on his cheek.

"But that is a lie, a lie to keep us from becoming the creatures that frightened your people in the first place.

When we use our magic for harm, we become stronger. I have more magic now than I did at the beginning of the war. At first, I could only use magic for languages. Now, I can do many things. Many unusual things."

He was pressed against the pole. Part of him wanted to stay and hear her out, while another part wanted to flee those dark eyes.

"How would I kill the Nazi butcher Hermann Göring? Like I killed the others. I would take his life from him with a slight touch, pull it out and extinguish it, so that no one would ever find its like again."

Cooper's mouth was dry. "You have to be close."

"I have to touch him," she said. "I had to touch all of them." And then she shuddered.

"Like you touched me?" he asked.

Her head tilted slightly. The hair fell away from her ears. They rose into slight points. He hadn't noticed that before.

"What do you mean?"

"If you can take, were you then giving so I felt strongly about you? So I'd take you to Nuremberg?"

She closed her eyes and backed away. Then she took a deep breath, opened her eyes and faced him.

"What was between us was real," she said. "I did not make it up."

"Not even to finish your assignment."

"It was not an assignment," she snapped. "It was revenge. I wanted them all dead. I wanted them all to die as horribly as my family did. As my friends. Can't you understand that?"

The pole was gouging into his back. He had seen what remained, what passed for life in those places. He could understand it, perhaps better than anyone else.

"If they had magic," he said, "why couldn't they get out?"

"I don't know," she said. "I expect some of them tried."

"And succeeded?"

She shrugged. "I will never know. Even if they lived, if they did not use violence, then they will not seek me out. I'm tainted now. I will be alone from now on."

He reached out. She watched as if she wasn't sure what he would do.

He wasn't sure until he took her hand in his shaking fingers.

"It's war," he said. "We do what we must in war. Surely they understand that."

"We are forbidden to fight for any reason," she said. "There are other ways to avoid capture, we're told. Other ways to avoid the violence."

'You don't believe it."

"Do you?" she asked. "Do you think this trial of yours will stop other criminals from trying to take over the world? Do you think this is anything but civilized revenge?"

He'd been trying not to think about it, but it nagged at him. It had been nagging at him from the start, getting worse at the camps, and made him wonder why someone didn't just shoot all the German leaders and have done with it.

"I've been trying to decide whether or not to stay," he said.

"In Paris?" she asked, with just a bit of hope in her voice. Just a bit, so small he wouldn't have heard it if he hadn't trained himself to listen to every inflection in every speech.

"In the military," he said. "I can reup for two more years."

"Why would you?"

"Civilized revenge."

Her hand slipped from his. He caught it again.

"But I'm tired," he said. "Finding translators could be my last assignment."

"Then you would go home."

He shook his head. "I don't really have one. I haven't lived anywhere longer than three months for the past ten years."

"But your family?"

"My parents," he said. "They don't need me. They have other children. They would be content to hear every now and then."

"So there is no place for you either," she said.

"I used to think maybe a university. I could teach languages and linguistic theory."

"It would be a good life."

"But why would they want a man who has done the things I have?"

"What have you done?" she asked.

"I have a gift for languages," he said, mimicking her phrase. "What do men with that gift do?"

"Listen," she said.

"And occasionally make people shut up."

She frowned, as if she didn't understand him. Then she laughed. The laugh surprised him. He had just confessed something to her he had told no one else, and she laughed at him.

"We are the same then," she said.

"No," he said. "I wish I could use touch. You have more finesse."

She stopped laughing, her smile fading. "You will not take me to Nuremberg."

"The war is over," he said. "I could stay here. With you."

"And what would we do?"

"Besides what we did last night?" he asked.

She nodded.

"We would listen," he said.

"And sometimes make people shut up?"

"I hope not," he said. "I hope it never comes to that again."

He kissed her. She kissed him back. Then she pulled away. "But humans have always been brutal, no?"

"Even when they fight for the right things," he said. "Are you human?"

"In all ways that matter," she said.

He nodded, not entirely understanding her. But, he just realized, he was going to take the time to find out what she meant. He was going back to headquarters and submit his resignation papers.

Finding the translators had been his last official job.

He would stay in Paris, with her, until he knew what was going to happen next.

Judgment

TYRONE STOPPED in front of the statue of Hans Sachs, which had somehow survived the bombings. The buildings around it had all been destroyed. No matter how hard Tyrone tried, he couldn't remember what they had been. The remains of a wall, two stories made of stone, suggested a church, but so many buildings in Nuremberg were made of stone that his impression was probably wrong.

The air smelled of dust, and beneath it, the faint hint of rot. He clutched his camera as he sat on a pile of rubble, the debris loose beneath his feet.

He had known Sachs, although the man did not look like his statue. The statue portrayed a robust figure, draped in robes and wearing medieval garb. The curly hair was right, but the artist failed to capture the thick brown tangles, and the beard was too neat, too well-trimmed.

Sachs had been too busy to be tidy.

Sachs, *Die Meistersinger von Nürnberg*. Amazing that Tyrone had forgotten Sachs. Sachs, after all, had been the one to lure him away from the forests and hills of his own people, had somehow started his strange romance with humans, and led to this moment, four centuries and a thousand lifetimes later.

Tyrone couldn't even remember what he had called himself in those early years. It hadn't been his own name—the magical never let anyone discover their true name. It gave others too much power.

Now he was calling himself Tyrone Briggs, although most of the people he encountered insisted on calling him Ty, a habit he hated, but never decried. He tried not to complain about anything American. He had learned after the First World War that not even Americans were safe from the kind of unreasoning patriotic fervor that made a man with a slight accent and an aversion to being called Ty suspect.

But those days were long past, just like that war was long past. This one was finally past too, but only by a few months.

And he hadn't expected to find himself on his native soil for the first time in forever.

The statue had not been here for all of those centuries. Hans Sachs would have been surprised to see it.

Die Meistersinger von Nürnberg. Tyrone shook his head. How had he forgotten that moment, when he'd hidden in the trees, and watched Sachs fiddle with his lute, trying to find the right words to go with a new melody, one that captured the exact sound of the wind in the leaves?

Tyrone had thought it a new magic, even though his father—a slight man with ears so pointed they poked through his long black hair—claimed it was no magic at all.

You are fooled by something that is not there. Humans only appear to have depth. They are fickle and violent and terrifying creatures. They will be the death of you.

But they hadn't been the death of Tyrone. He had not become mortal, and they had not discovered him. He had passed for generations. So many generations, in fact, that Tyrone had come to think of Sachs not as the man he knew, but as the title character in Wagner's opera *Die Meistersinger*, the opera that had always been performed before the annual Nazi rallies held in Nuremberg, an opera he had always hated.

Tyrone shuddered, even though it was not that cold. The thin November sun filtered through the rubble, back-lighting the crumbling walls, peeking through the falling doorways.

Nuremberg had been a medieval city, with its ancient wall still intact. The castle, Kaiserburg, stood on a sandstone crag above the wall. When Tyrone had first come here, the castle had seemed a lone outpost, the guardian of the city. Over the centuries, it had become part of the city—a talisman, guarding the place.

Now it was a ghost, windows shattered, walls fallen, an entire section gone. Tyrone had thought some human things timeless. This war, more than the last, had proven him wrong.

He clutched the camera, knowing he should photograph the devastation. That was what he was here for—he was supposed to photograph the trials, which would start in a few days, and he was supposed to photograph the city, which had suffered a devastating Allied attack, second only to the bombing of Dresden in loss of German civilian life.

It would cheer the Americans to see this—the good Ole U.S. of A. loved the destruction. It made them feel virtuous. Nuremberg had been the center of Nazism. The frightening newsreels of Adolf Hitler waving his small fist and shouting at the top of his scarred lungs at hundreds upon hundreds of jack-booted Nazis had come from here, from Zeppelin Field, which was not in the old city, but the new. Or what had been the new.

That's why the trials were being held here. To show the world that the Allies had won. To prove to the surviving Axis citizens that destruction awaited anyone who crossed the United States, Great Britain and Russia. Or maybe not Russia. Not any more.

That alliance had been one of convenience, already collapsing.

Tyrone sighed and stood. Human interactions. Human thoughts. He had abandoned his magic in this city, lifetimes ago and had embraced everything human. He last used his powers to round his ears and his eyes, to straighten his eyebrows and to dull his teeth. When he had done that, he had sacrificed his feral beauty—something which marked him as Other. But a spark of it remained. If he wanted to, he could attract a woman with a simple smile and the glimmer of an eye. He could make men—some men—remain at his side for life, ever loyal.

He could bewitch anyone he wanted for as long as he wanted.

But he hadn't done those things in centuries either.

The sunlight was fading. He stood, photographs untaken, the image of Hans Sachs—as he had been, not as he had been immortalized—burned into Tyrone's brain.

And the music, nearly forgotten, whispering, whispering—like a faraway wind through a pile of dead, dry leaves.

***

TYRONE HAD LIVED through two of what his people called cycles—near as he could figure 200 years in human time—and had been betrothed to a woman with a far more savage beauty than his own. Her family's magic was legendary; their penchant for mischief even more so. The sagas he later learned from human troubadours—sagas of stolen infants, mistaken identities, and chilled souls—all came from her family, with its courage, and willingness to challenge the humans.

Tyrone had watched the humans long before his betrothal. At first, he thought them a dirty, loutish lot, and could not understand why his people insisted on co-existing with them.

He had been less than half a cycle when he asked his father why the People had not made humans into slaves.

His father had studied him for a long time, as if he had asked a forbidden question, and then had said, *We have magic. They have strength.*

And no matter how much more Tyrone asked, he never got a more satisfactory answer than that.

His people lived in a half-world, a twist away from the world humans called real. The People built their own castles out of air, hiding them inside forests of tall, ancient trees, and believing the cities safe. Sometimes a youngling emerged from the forest, living among the humans as a rite of passage. If discovered, the youngling returned in shame, destined to be one of the Low Folk. If the deception had been successful, the youngling became one of the High Folk, the rulers, the aristocracy of the People, those who decided it all.

His betrothed's family always participated in the rite. She had, and seemed appalled when she learned that he had not. No one in his family had passed for human in several cycles.

Why take the risk, his father had asked, *when our family's place among the High Folk remains guaranteed thanks to the deceptions of our ancestors?*

Perhaps Tyrone had ventured out that day because of his betrothed's taunting. Sometimes he thought it nothing more than that. Then he remembered the suffocating feeling he had whenever he participated in the People's rituals, the knowledge that for twenty cycles, maybe more, he would do the same things, be bound to the same woman, and live on the same land.

There had to be more to life than magic classes in which he graduated to ever more elaborate spells, spells designed to create fancy palaces or beautiful clothing or marvelous pranks with which to entrance the humans. Most of the People loved these games, and found them endlessly fascinating. Some specialized in various parts of the magic—like his betrothed's family in Passing and Pranks, and his own in Light Weaving and the Architecture of Air.

But Tyrone's mind was restless—undisciplined, his father said—and he wanted to use his magic in the old ways, outside the prescribed laws and rules.

He had tried that only once—a simple spell, changing leaf color before the fall—and his punishment had been severe. No magic for a dozen seasons, and then, when the ban was lifted, only supervised spells. He had been watched over as if he had slaughtered a unicorn, and even though the incident was five seasons in the past when he became betrothed, he had not forgotten it.

He doubted he ever would.

But other younglings felt dissatisfaction with the People. None had fled before. None had spent their entire lives among the humans.

Tyrone often thought his dissatisfaction a symptom of something more, of a part of him no one spoke of, a part only hinted at. For no one mentioned his mother, and the People were famed for seducing—and abandoning—human girls, only to steal their infants later.

Tyrone suspected that his restless "undisciplined" mind may have had another source, one his family was not willing to acknowledge—one that had given him a fascination with things human that the People could never ever understand.

***

THE PRESS CORPS had its own buildings near the Palace of Justice because the world wanted this trial reported. Tyrone had already met two newsreel photographers who planned to record the entire event on film. He felt almost redundant—a still photographer in a world that was starting to move.

At least he didn't have to put everything together like the print guys, who would be writing not just about the daily events, but trying to make some sense of the atrocities that would be brought as evidence.

Tyrone had seen none of that material, and he didn't want to see it, although he would have to as part of his job. He had been sent here as principal photographer for a major New York daily, thanks to his own stupidity and an argument he had had with his editor.

Tyrone had spent most of the war in the States—too old to fight (even in his human identity), and unwilling to tromp through Europe and Asia chasing stories with bombs exploding around him.

He had almost succeeded. He would have succeeded if he had kept his big mouth shut.

Instead, he had argued with a co-worker, telling him that Hitler had not been a mustachioed buffoon as he was presented in the American papers, but a real threat. It had been clear, Tyrone had said, from the moment Hitler's first speeches had aired in the 1930s. Anyone with even a passing understanding of German and the German mind should have realized the danger that Hitler presented.

Of course, Tyrone's editor had overheard that and had expressed surprise that Tyrone knew German or the German mind. Then he remembered Tyrone's phony application, which claimed he was an American raised in Europe, and decided that what the paper needed was, quite simply, a fresh perspective on the war, from someone who hadn't experienced it.

No matter how many arguments Tyrone made, he couldn't prevent the trip to the city he sometimes like to imagine he had been born in, for it was the place when he became truly human, a city he hadn't returned to in hundreds of years.

He had been among the humans so long that it took until he reached the reporters wing in the compound around the Palace of Justice to realize that he could have argued with his boss or simply quit.

Instead, he had come to Nuremberg like a puppet, determined to find the photographs that best represented each day's trial highlight.

So far, he hadn't taken many. He hadn't even seen the prisoners—Goring, Hess, and all the rest—the admirals, and generals, and others that had been captured because Hitler had been too cowardly to face his enemies. Even if Tyrone had seen the prisoners, he wasn't sure if he would take their pictures.

Since he had come to Nuremberg, his interest in photography had faded.

That very first night, as he lay in the army issue cot, in a room so narrow that it felt like a cell, he had dreamed of his own past. Sneaking over the ancient wall, going to Sachs's cobbler's shop, and listening for the music, convinced that it was something more than even his people could do.

In the dream, Tyrone had spoken to Sachs, but in life, they had never had a conversation. Tyrone had merely listened to Sachs's music, and tried to learn, thinking music beyond him.

Later, he realized that Sachs would have helped him, that the Meistersingers believed that their art was a trade, as simple as shoe-making, and that anyone could have trained in it.

But Tyrone had thought it magic, and had approached it as such, believing that innate ability counted for more than sheer drive and willingness. The People had no musical traditions—he didn't know what songs were until he had emerged from the forest, and he certainly hadn't understood instruments—so he had had nothing to build on.

Just as he had had nothing to build on when he had tried his hand at other human "magics"—painting, and sculpture, and the creation of books. Over the generations, he had tried most of the human art forms, and they had all failed him.

Until photography. The combination of light and shadow, the ability to frame the world into single images, accented his family's real magic—their manipulation of light, their willingness to create buildings out of air.

In his dream, he had gone back to Sachs' cobbler shop with a camera, trying to photograph the music that had drawn him from the woods, but he had been unable to do so. Too much time had passed; he had learned too much—realized that Sachs, like most of the other Meistersingers, had left no lasting legacy, not like Bach or Beethoven or Mozart. Their legacy had been composition and genius and true music. Sachs, while gifted, had followed the guidelines of his trade: he had rarely composed his own melodies, and his lyrics—his pride and joy—had been instructional stories, not cries from his heart.

Tyrone had awakened from that dream shaken and spent. The feelings that rose within him—the fear, the longing, the loneliness—seemed as real as they had all those years ago.

He blamed the dream on Nuremberg itself—on the distinctive sparkle of the Pegnitz River, on the shadow of Kaiserburg falling across the destroyed city of his past, on the stench of the unburied bodies still lying beneath the rubble—bringing to mind the first deaths he had seen, shortly after he had arrived in the city and learned that humans were not immortal.

The city brought out a disquiet in him, a disquiet he hadn't felt since he had first taken a camera in his hands seventy years before. The nearness of his past, combined with the feeling of violence still shuddering in the air, awakened a part of him that had been dormant too long.

The trial was not set to start for another day or two, and his only assignment was to photograph the city, give the readers a sense of the setting for what his editor called one of the most important moments in human history.

Other photographers were already getting shots of the ruins, of the hollow-faced children, of the women, heads bowed in defeat.

He wasn't interested in any of that.

Since he returned here, he was interested in only one thing. Home.

***

Which was how he found himself, threading his way through Nuremberg, trying to compare the topology of his memory with the destruction before him. The cobblestone streets had been cleared so that Army jeeps could make their way through, looking official and abnormally clean in the late fall sunlight.

Tyrone wore his favorite boots beneath khaki pants and a warm bomber jacket over all of it. His hair was tucked into a stocking cap and he had gloves in his pocket. He also brought a flask filled with water, three candy bars—as precious as gold here—and his camera.

The camera seemed like a drag on him; extra weight he thought of leaving behind more than once. But each time he set it down, he couldn't let go of it, and finally he put the strap around his neck, letting the camera hang, heavy and solid, against his chest.

Nuremberg seemed to go on forever. Once he passed the wall, he entered the new city, with its curving streets and burned homes. They had been made of wood, not stone, and the conflagration must have been horrible.

He saw no people here, no lost children, no sad women. Only the occasional shoe and scrawny dog, poking its face in the ruins. More than one of these half-wild dogs chewed on things they had found beneath the ashes; he did not stop to see what that was.

Instead, he walked and walked and walked, and knew he had never walked this far as a young man. He supposed he could have looked at a map—if he could find one—or asked one of the locals, if they would deign to talk to him.

But he did not. Instead, he followed the bend of the river, knowing it would take him to the outskirts of the city eventually.

It took half of the day to reach the edge of the city, half of the day and two of his three candy bars. There were only a few hours of light left when he stepped onto the bombed-out road, and looked down the slight hill into the clearing beyond.

No trees. That was the first thing he noticed. No trees, and little growth. The brown earth had been churned up by vehicles and bomb craters and scavengers.

This was not the land of his memory. There were no forests, no birds, no green—only destruction as far as his eye could see.

For a long time, he stood on the slight rise, feeling his heart pound. The breath burned in his lungs—he wasn't used to walking any longer—and his muscles shook.

He hadn't expected to find the People, not when he had started on this trip, but he had thought he would catch a hint of them, a flash of light in the trees—the hint of a building against the clouds.

He hadn't expected to find them, but he had hoped he would—even imagined it: Ducking into the trees, speaking the old words, having the world twist ever so slightly—and then he would be in the sky.

His father, a touch of silver in his thick dark hair, would praise him. *You have extended the family honor,* he would have said. *We will be among the High Folk for several more generations.*

And Tyrone would sit on the Throne of Success, telling all about his adventures, showing them the camera and explaining its ability to capture light, singing to them a bit of Brahms' Lullaby, and attempting to explain the purpose of art.

Some wouldn't have believed him, of course. They would think that he hid during his tenure, that he had seen nothing, participated in nothing. They wouldn't know of the human women he had tried to love, the friends he could never quite get close to, the judgments he had formed about a life that would mean nothing inside those gossamer walls.

He would have gone back, and once back, he would have to decide if he wanted to stay, decide if now he was ready to do the same things, be bound to the same woman, and live on the same land.

But, he realized now, it wasn't going to be that easy. He stood on the rise and stared at the destroyed land, knowing that he would never go home—at least not the home of his youth.

He had been wrong. He would not have lived in the same place for all of his cycles. He would have moved on, to somewhere else that humans hadn't invaded, a place that still had greenery, trees, and a bit of water.

Because his people had to have moved on. They had survived other human destructions—wars that lasted decades, horrible diseases that sometimes transferred to the magical, terrible fires that destroyed all of the surrounding countryside. But this time something had happened, something which made them find new ground.

But they would be close, and he would find them.

Although he wouldn't find them on this day. He had weeks now. Weeks of a trial which the humans thought would make everything better. Just like the previous war was a war to end all wars. Just like the way Europe thought it was through with dictators when Napoleon was banished to Elba.

Tyrone didn't know how long he was standing there before he lifted his camera. He didn't know how long he shot before he realized he was taking pictures.

Capturing the present in light and shadow, making memories out of air.

***

By the time he returned to his small room, he had a plan. He would talk to the locals, find out if there were examples of pranks played in the last generation—maybe even on the Nazis themselves.

There would be stories—there were always stories—of a haunted wood, visions of light against darkness. Stories of drunken men taken to buildings in the clouds, only to return years later. Stories of women seduced by men of great beauty, only to have the children of those unions stolen in the middle of the night.

He would find his people.

At least, he hoped he would.

***

Two weeks into the trial, he had gotten nowhere. The locals would not talk to him, seeing him as the enemy—one of the destroyers. They seemed to have no concept of their own guilt—in believing in the filth that Hitler had spoken—that brought this disaster upon themselves.

Photographs were not allowed during testimony and arguments, unless they were taken without flash from a great distance. So Tyrone rarely stayed for the entire day, preferring to photograph the justices as they gaveled the session to order, or the witnesses as they climbed into the box.

He specialized in candid shots—a young guard, smoking outside the Palace of Justice, a soldier standing at rigid attention against the doors leading into Room Number 600, a young boy staring at the curtained windows of the east wing, allowing no one to see inside.

His editor proclaimed himself pleased—*You have an artist's eye, Tyrone,* he had said during an expensive international call. *Keep doing what you're doing. No one else is getting this stuff.*

Everyone else was running in packs, trying to be journalists, when the work of journalists was long past.

Tyrone was walking the streets of Nuremberg, familiarizing himself with the city that the Allies once considered bulldozing before they fixed it up.

He finally found himself on Zeppelin Field. Bombs had cratered it, but the marble stands still remained. He could almost hear the roar of the crowd, feel the vibrations from a thousand jack-boots hitting the earth in unison.

There was an electricity here, a sick and dangerous magic, one that lingered, like the scent of rot in the air.

It was December, and the light was fading early. Even at midday, there was a twilight sort of darkness to the city and no sense of merriment. Germans, who had loved the pagan holiday their priests had confiscated for Christ, were not celebrating this year.

They had nothing to celebrate, nothing at all.

Tyrone was wondering how he could photograph this, how he could catch not just the weeds and craters in the field that once held the flower of Nazi youth, but the sense of illness here, of a twisted and decaying ideology that had somehow captured an entire people.

And then he saw her, huddled in rags against one of the benches, watching him.

She was slender to the point of gauntness, her clothing in rags. Her hair, midnight black, was tangled over her face, but he didn't need to see it.

The magic sparkled off her like the aftermath of a flashbulb's light.

He did not try to photograph her. He knew it would be useless. At best, he would get a collection of rags. At worst, a ruined film with none of his pictures saved.

Instead, he let his camera hang around his neck as he walked toward her, slowly enough to let her flee if she felt she had to.

As he approached, she pushed her hair away from her face. Her savage beauty remained, perhaps even stronger now that no fat lined her bones.

"I thought it was you," she said, her voice huskier than he remembered. She spoke an Old German, one he barely understood. "You look like them."

He could not remember her name, even though they had been betrothed. Like his own, he had not thought of it in centuries. And now she probably blocked it from his mind so that he would have no power over her.

He sat beside her, the marble cold through his wool pants. "I came looking for you," he said.

"Not me." She gave him a small smile, and he was grateful that it was small. He no longer had defenses against even the slightest magic. "You wanted to be the conquering hero, just like those you've emulated for so long."

He almost denied it, and then he remembered his fantasy—sitting on the Throne of Success, extending his family's honor, becoming one of the High Folk for all of eternity.

"It's like a disease, isn't it? Some kind of infection that gets passed from creature to creature. Now you have it." She shook her magnificent head, then gazed across the empty expanse of field. "And look where it got them."

He started when he realized that she thought he empathized with the Nazis. He wondered if she knew what was going on across town, how Hitler's henchmen were just beginning to find out there was no justification for their crimes.

Her eyes glittered as she watched him, and they made him even more uneasy. There was a great intelligence in them, but nothing else.

He had never loved her—the People did not speak of love, thinking it a human invention—but he had been bound to her, by tradition and fascination and a common heritage.

It all felt so long ago.

"My father?" Tyrone asked. "How do I find him?"

She looked down, smoothed her rags as if they were a gown made of silk. Then she shook her head.

"I can't find him?" Tyrone asked. "Because of what I've become?"

She shook her head again.

"He can't be dead." Tyrone's voice shook. "The People do not die."

"Did not die," she said. "But all things have an end—."

She almost said his name then—his true name—but she caught herself just in time. He could feel it, hovering between them, before it vanished.

"The People can't be dead," he said. "You're not."

She shrugged. "Dead, scattered, destroyed. Even we had no defense from fire that rains from the sky, burning the trees and sucking away the air. Some of us managed to escape, only to be discovered and taken…hideous places. Hideous."

She shuddered, lost in memory.

Then he heard his father's voice, as clear as if the man had been beside him. *We have magic. They have strength.*

Had his father foreseen this? The craters, the destruction, the rubble? Had his father known?

"Why did you reveal yourself to me?" Tyrone asked.

She brushed her hair away from her face again, and this time, her smile was soft. She put her hand on his cheek, and her skin was cold. Not the cold of a person who had sat too long in the December twilight, but the cold of marble, of something that had no life at all.

"Because," she said, "it is rare to get the chance to say good-bye."

And then she vanished, leaving only a swirl of air. He reached for her, knowing that she hadn't moved, but he could not find her. He recited the old words, but she did not come back.

He sat on the marble seats long into the growing dark. But the only ghosts that surrounded him marched in unison under what they believed to be a bright, sunlight sky. He could not banish them, and he could not photograph them.

Not that he really wanted to try.

***

HE SEARCHED for the next two hundred days, while he listened to testimony about atrocities that shocked even his ancient spirit. He befriend a few locals, but heard only sad stories of beautiful people in rags, of lights exploding against the darkness as if hit with invisible grenades, of a sense of loss so deep that it seemed to come from the earth itself.

And finally, finally, the trial ended, and he was able to go home—although not the place he had meant by home all those months before. He was an American raised in Europe, a Europe that no longer existed, if it ever had. A Europe as misremembered as Hans Sachs had been, a Meistersinger that may not have been a master singer at all.

***

YEARS LATER, Tyrone was going through his old photographs, looking at the best of the unpublished ones for a history book he had been hired to illustrate, when he found the shots he had taken that afternoon early in the trials, the afternoon he had walked to the edge of town with only three candy bars, a flask of water, and his camera.

Wisps of light appeared at the edge of the exposures, hints of turrets rising in the air. It took him a while, but he eventually located the negatives and made new prints.

The wisps were in every one.

The People were still there. They had seen him, sensed his thoughts, and had judged him unworthy.

So they had sent her, his betrothed, a woman whose family specialized in Passing and Pranks, to test him.

She had fooled the human, just like her family had done for generations.

Fooled the human, and once again maintained her position among the High Folk.

He smiled. From their perspective, he had failed.

But from his, he had not.

For in the past two cycles since he had been gone, nothing among the People had changed.

Nothing, that is, except him.

The Thrill of the Hunt

S HE HID ALONG the lowest ridge, feet sprawled, extended downhill. She had rolled in the dirt, covering herself and her clothing, her hair buried under a dirt-covered hat, so that she blended in. Her only risk—the binoculars. They could glint in the sun, warning him.

The sun was hot. Powerfully hot. She hadn't expected it. She had been in Northern Europe too long with its pale sunlight and cool summers. She had never been to Argentina before.

She shifted ever so slightly, measuring the distance with her eyes. He had moved to a dilapidated farmhouse, the wood gray and sagging from the harsh weather. Grime covered the windows.

If she hadn't known, if she hadn't followed him here, she would have thought the place abandoned.

He lived here. The Great Wulf, who had once lived in a lavish castle overlooking the Rhine, had settled in this dry and dusty place, living in near poverty.

She wouldn't have believed it if she hadn't seen it for herself. She tracked him here, watched him enter that ruined building. He looked like so many German exiles in this part of Argentina, back bowed, too thin, defeated.

They shouldn't have seemed so defeated, these German exiles. They escaped.

The binoculars were heavy, and they yielded little. The crookedly hung front door. The broken stoop. Empty chicken coops.

The farm clearly did not sustain itself and the Great Wulf did nothing to change that. He hadn't tilled the land or hired anyone to help him. He kept no animals, and he appeared to live alone.

But she had no way of telling what lurked behind that door.

She didn't want to go in. Once she went in, she would be at his mercy. She would stay outside and kill him the hard way.

With a rifle.

And, with luck, he would never know what hit him.

***

IN THE END, she had volunteered.

She found that ironic now, that she had volunteered. She had learned he was in Argentina, and she saw it, not as an opportunity for vengeance, but as a way out of Europe.

Europe, so defeated, so destroyed. Everywhere she went, she found rubble, starving people, begging children. She could not help them. She did not want to help them, if the truth be told.

She used to have compassion, back before two world wars destroyed it. Or perhaps it wasn't the wars, but the aftermaths. When she met a single starving person, she gave money or food or helped the poor soul find shelter.

When she saw dozens, she turned away.

But now that there were thousands—thin ragged near-corpses—she felt only irritation. Irritation at them for failing to provide for themselves somehow (even though she knew so many of them couldn't), irritation at the remains of the governments for ignoring the problem, irritation at the combatants for causing this problem in the first place.

Someone else needed to solve the crisis. She could not. She *would* not.

She had survived, first by hiding, then by pretending to be one of them. She was blond. She had blue eyes and high cheekbones. She stole the identity of a German woman and lived part of the war in Paris, where a semblance of a civilization remained.

She stayed through the liberation with yet another piece of identification, this one marking her as French (her language skills were good enough, as long as she told people she was from the Alsace). She might have stayed there, if it weren't for the dreams.

***

THE FARM'S ISOLATION worked for her and worked against her. With her hair beneath the hat, loose clothing, and dirt all over her face, she could pass for a boy. The problem was that everyone in this little valley seemed to know everyone else.

Things would have been much easier had Wulf still lived in Buenos Aires.

She had parked her old Ford pickup over a mile away on what was little more than a cart path. The roads here were dirt, harsh, uncompromising. The side roads looked like they were created by rabbits.

She had found just enough brush to shield the truck from the most overt gaze, but it would not remain hidden for long. Someone would see it. Someone would report it. Someone would find her.

No movement inside the farmhouse. Nothing outside as well, although she did not expect it, in the heat of the day like this.

She was foolish, lying in the sun like this, with only her binoculars and two old Coke bottles filled with water.

She would need to plan better when she came to do her job.

She would need food, a bit of shade (and there was none, not within range), and enough water to make it for more than a day. If only she could wait until the weather cooled, and the rains started.

But then she would have the water to deal with, and probably the wind.

Plus there would be no guarantee that he would remain here.

No guarantee that he wouldn't sense her.

No guarantee that he wouldn't kill her.
Like he had killed so many before.

***

THE FIRST DREAM seemed benign. Her father, sitting in his favorite chair, a worn red velvet chair her mother wanted to replace. Her father had had kind eyes and silver hair. In the dream, he held his pipe, puffing it occasionally, filling the room with the scent of his specially blended tobacco.

She had awakened in tears, still smelling the tobacco, still feeling the warmth of the room.

She missed him. She had never mourned him or her mother. She had moved on—she had to, or she would have died—but now, in the comfort of her Parisian bed, in the first winter after the war (the second war), she felt herself shivering from loss.

If she let in that loss, she would have to let in all the others, and she would collapse. She would never be able to move, never be able to function.

She fled Paris for Venice because she heard that it too was untouched.

But that was a lie. Venice looked the same—no one had bombed its lovely bridges. The canals smelled as ripe as they always had—but the winter was cold and damp and no one had money. So many exiles in that place, so many formerly wealthy Europeans trying to find the life they had had between the wars, mourning what they had lost.

It drizzled when she arrived and it drizzled when she left. She had been cold the entire time she was in Venice and she finally decided to go home.

To Germany.

***

SHE STAYED LOW to the ground as she hurried along the ridgeline, watching the road for any signs of anyone. She headed back to the truck.

The silence in the valley was vast. She now knew that when she started that truck's engine, people would be able to hear it for miles.

The valley was narrower than it looked, or perhaps the tall mountains simply reined in sound. Or the heat, accompanied by the unbearably thick humidity, caused some kind of acoustical feedback.

She didn't know.

But it posed yet another risk, in a job filled with risks.

She wasn't sure how she would solve them yet.

Or if she could solve them.

All she knew was that she felt compelled to try.

***

WHEN SHE DECIDED to return to Germany, her first thought was how bad could it be? Sure, she had read the reports of the Allied bombings. She knew that some areas had become craters. She knew that Dresden was gone.

She toyed with going to Munich—her family had lived there for a generation, but that was the generation before hers. She barely remembered the city. She wanted to see Berlin.

She had grown up in a tree-lined neighborhood, in a big rambling house, with fireplaces in each bedroom, and a massive double fireplace on the first floor. Her parents never shut the front parlor, not even in the winter, because they could afford the wood to keep the place heated.

As she edged toward adulthood, she would tease her father, saying he had used some sort of alchemy to make the wood last. He hadn't denied it.

But later, she realized it wasn't the wood he had magicked. He paid for the wood, like he paid for most things.

He never touched the wood. But he used his own brand of magic on the heat, moving it from floor to floor, keeping the entire house warm, when the homes of her friends always had cold spots and closed unheated rooms.

She had been raised in a wealthy household, a scholarly household, and she had taken the comfort for granted.

She had taken it all for granted—the clothing, the rich food, her parents as they laughed late at night.

A child raised in love, her mother used to say, *will always be able to love in return.*

Perhaps, once upon a time, her mother had been right. But her mother had no idea what the future was going to bring them.

Her mother, who would die screaming, blood oozing from the pores in her skin.

Her mother, who would plead for the lives of all four of her children.

Her mother, who, when offered the chance to save one, would refuse to save any at all.

***

EVEN WITH THE WINDOWS OPEN, the truck was too hot. She wrapped her shirttail around her hand just so that she could grab the door handle, feeling the metal sear into her palm as she tugged.

She didn't relish the drive back. The open windows would merely blow the hot air around, not cool it off.

She had no idea how anyone lived down here, why anyone lived down here, how they survived the summers or why they even tried.

Christmas had been the worst. She hadn't expected it. She never thought of Christmas in a tropical place, on the wrong side of the equator, where summer and winter were reversed.

She liked the cold, the snow, the dismal gray sky. She hadn't been prepared for the unrelenting heat and the glaring sunshine.

It was on Christmas morning—less than a month ago now—that she realized the Germans here truly were exiles. No self-respecting German would celebrate Christmas in a place like this, not voluntarily, not year after year after year.

She drove back to Buenos Aires in a half crouch as she waited for the bench seat to cool off. It was too hot to sit on, at least for a long period of time, and she thought about that as well.

Maybe she was making the wrong plans because she was in a foreign place, a place so strange to her that she felt on edge just by being here. The heat in December and January, a kind of heat she had never experienced before, the roads that seemed more like paths, the dirt and the dust and the faint smell of manure, coming from the various farms all around her.

In the city, she smelled only exhaust. The buildings, which someone had once described to her as having an old-world charm, did not look old-world to her. She had come from the old world, the very old world, and the buildings there had had a real charm.

Part of Buenos Aires had been built in an old world style, but with new world materials—woods that were unfamiliar to her—and painted a brilliant white so that they withstood the sun.

In the Mediterranean, when the locals used white, they painted it on brick or stone. They knew that stone kept the heat out.

The wood did not.

But, she was told, it grew cold in Buenos Aires during the winter—a damp cold, the kind that seeped into your bones. And the wooden houses were supposed to be good at dealing with that kind of cold. A local had told her that the stone held in the dampness, while the wood let it escape.

She did not know. She hoped she wouldn't have to find out.

By the time she reached Buenos Aires, the truck's seat had cooled enough to allow her to sit. She drew strange looks with her dusty truck, her dirty face, and her filthy clothing. But she ignored them. She knew people thought they were looking at a boy. No self-respecting woman dressed like she did.

Later, when she left her apartment, she would dress in a flared skirt and light blouse, her hair combed around her face, and her make-up just so. Down here, the locals favored bright red lipstick with a touch of rouge, and often they accented their eyes with a hint of kohl.

She was too fair to use kohl and if she used too much rouge, she looked like a German kewpie doll. But if she applied the make-up properly, she looked less German and more American. Her Spanish wasn't good enough to make her sound like an Argentinean no matter how hard she tried. Her fluency in French and Italian actually hurt her assimilation. The words in all three languages were too similar and at times, they confused her. She had to speak slowly so that she would say the exact right things.

When she finally arrived at her apartment in one of the poorer sections of the city, she looked at no one. People didn't look at her either. But she knew what they thought, if they thought of her at all.

They thought the dust-covered boy in the truck was the brother of the woman who had rented the apartment. She made sure they thought this. Otherwise, she never would have rented in a neighborhood like this.

The apartment came with a small garage. She deliberately looked for a place with a garage because, after seeing the poverty in the outskirts of the city, she did not want to leave the truck on the street.

The apartment and garage cost her more than a simple apartment would, but it had the benefit of placing her in a slightly better neighborhood. She didn't care about the money. She had more than enough and her sponsors would give her even more if she asked.

But she wasn't going to contact anyone, not until the job was done.

They had hired her, yes, for an obscene amount of money.

But she would have done the job for free if she had been able to find Wulf on her own. She hadn't been able to.

She had needed her sponsors. They had tracked down Wulf. They had come up with the plan.

She had had no plan, not until 1947 when the dreams became unbearable.

***

In Paris, she dreamed of her father, always awakening to the scent of pipe smoke. For a while, she had thought one of her neighbors smoked the same special blend of tobacco, bringing the dreams, but the dreams followed her to Venice, and she knew then and there that they were coming from another place—although she wasn't sure if they came from inside herself or from someone else, attempting to trigger memories.

But the dreams expanded in Venice, changed just enough that she realized they were dreams.

Her father would smoke and smile, leaning back in his chair as he contemplated something important.

Her mother sang as she set the formal dining room table. Their housekeeper would try to stop her mother from working, but her mother would have none of it. She liked to be useful, she said, and since she married, she hadn't felt useful.

Her siblings rarely made an appearance. In some of the dreams, she felt like an only child.

She woke in tears from those dreams as well. Because she was an only child.

Now.

In the dreams, she would lean her head on her father's knee. He would put a hand on her head.

Such a comforting gesture. Such a comforting dream. The pipe smoke, the singing, the warmth of his hand.

And then it all changed.

The library got cold, damp, and it smelled fetid. The stink of the canals invaded her dreams.

Until one night, her father leaned forward, his eyes so blue they barely looked human. She had seen him like that only a few times in her life, and the look always sparked fear in her.

It sparked fear in the dreams as well.

"Hilda," he said, and she cringed at the sound of her name. She had abandoned that name when she fled her dying family. She took whatever name anyone gave her now, and she lived by that name until the name was no longer useful.

But Hilda, she had been Hilda to her family, to those she loved.

Those she failed.

And those who failed her.

She would force herself awake after he spoke her name, his voice echoing in her ears. She would walk to the window and look out at the chill, sleeping city, only a few lights burning, and she would remind herself that her family was long dead, her parents were long dead.

She owed no one anything.

But she did not believe it.

She breathed.

She stood.

She lived.

They did not.

And at some point, she knew, she would have to do something about that.

***

HER BUENOS AIRES APARTMENT came furnished. The kitchen smelled of cooking oils, chilies, and garlic, old lingering odors that no amount of scrubbing could erase.

The sofa sagged, but the mattress in the one and only bedroom was firm—relatively new, which made her wonder what had happened to the old one. In places like this, the owners did not replace the furniture unless it had become useless.

Sometimes, as she lay in the heat, the windows open and the city sounds echoing around her, she wondered if the person who held the apartment before her had been elderly, and if he had died in this bed.

Although it would not have been this bed. It would have been another.

To die in this heat would leave an odor, worse than the garlic, chili, and cooking oils smell of the kitchen. So either no one died here, or the dead body was found relatively soon.

Perhaps something else had happened to the mattress. Perhaps the previous tenant had stolen it.

Perhaps the springs had finally poked through.

It was a measure of her life that she though of death first, rancid putrid death, which was what she had found in Berlin.

Ragged people, the stench of death.

A city she no longer recognized.

A place she had to escape.

But she had not known that when she arrived in Berlin.

When she arrived, she thought she was following the compulsion of the dreams.

She thought she was doing what she needed to do to get a little peace.

***

"HILDA," HER FATHER SAID, "he is still alive."

She didn't have to ask who "he" was. She knew. With the logic of dreams, she knew her father was speaking of the Great Wulf, even though she hadn't heard of the Great Wulf until her father was already dead.

At Wulf's hand.

Then she'd been hauled into his castle—his lair, he'd said laughing—and propped against a wall with her siblings. Her brother Gunther, all of three. Her sister, Lisel, eight. Her other sister, Eda, twelve. She squeezed between them. Hilda, fourteen.

Still, he hadn't looked at her, the Great Wulf. Thin, austere, with dark hair and dark malevolent eyes. His lips were thin, his beard a mere wisp on his chin. His clothing matched his hair, as brown as the wooden chairs, his skin as gray as the walls.

He did not seem healthy. Hilda had difficulty thinking of him as strong. As powerful enough to murder her father, with little more than a thought.

But he had.

She had seen it.

She had seen it all.

Wulf watched her mother. Her mother, still beautiful, still relatively young. All of her children shared her blond hair, her fair skin. The younger three had her brown eyes. But Hilda had her father's blue eyes, which she took a care to shield.

Their fire hadn't saved her father. They had flashed so blue, she thought he would bring the world down around them. But he hadn't had that kind of power. His gifts were domestic, gentle, built for comfort, not for destruction.

Wulf destroyed comfort, loathed it. Saw it as a threat. She sensed that the moment she walked into his castle, saw the sharp edges, and felt the chill. The most powerful man of his age, and he kept his home cold and unwelcoming.

Especially this cellar, deep beneath the mountain, no windows, nothing except a stout oak door. Eda whispered that perhaps it had been a prison once. A cell, Lisel had corrected.

Her mother had begged them to hush. She had had no powers, always relying on her husband's, and now he was dead.

Wulf had brought her mother here, not because she was special, but because she wasn't. Because he could. He loved tormenting people. He adored tormenting her.

He had tormented her mother alone for days. When the servants brought the children into the cell, Hilda expected to see a broken disheveled version of her mother. Instead, her mother looked as she had before—her dress neat, her feet crossed at the ankles and tucked at the side of the chair, her hair pulled back into a soft bun.

Only her eyes were different. Older. Sadder. Almost empty.

Until she saw the children.

Nooooo, she had moaned.

No.

The word echoed against the damp stone walls. The entire cell smelled of mildew and sweat, a scent Hilda would later associate with fear.

Perhaps that was why she had hated Venice. The smell of mildew. The remains of fear.

Thoughts like that would jolt her awake every single time. The dream would end, but the memory wouldn't. She would roll over in bed, wrap a pillow around her head, try to blunt the thoughts, the recollections, but she couldn't.

She couldn't.

They would come anyway, all of them, flashing through her mind like a broken film.

Wulf sweeping his hand toward the children he had lined against the wall. *You can live,* he said, *if you chose which three of your children must die.*

Gunther, crying. Mama. Mama. Wanting to run to her.

Lisel, holding him back.

Their mother, shaking her head.

Choose, Wulf said. *You will live.*

Mother, shaking her head.

Then they will all die, Wulf said, *and you will still live.*

Hilda meeting her gaze. Her mother's eyes filled with tears. *Let me die,* she said. *Let them live.*

Hilda should have shielded them long before they had been brought to the castle. She should have herded them out of the house, down the tree-lined street, into the vastness of Berlin itself. She should have taken them far, far away.

But she hadn't known that then. She hadn't known what was possible. She hadn't known what she could do.

Her eyes warmed.

Her mother panicked, shook her head slightly, the gesture aimed at Hilda, not at Wulf. Later, Hilda would recognize the feeling, know what it meant. Her blue, blue eyes had flared, like her father's used to, when he touched his powers.

She had finally found hers.

Too late.

But she had no idea what they were or how to use them.

Her mother slowly closed her eyes, giving Hilda an example, silently telling her to look down, away, keep her own eyes shielded.

Only one with power, Wulf said, without turning around. *Sad how families work, isn't it? The traits you want to give your children aren't always the traits they get.*

Mama, Gunther wailed. Mama.

Lisel pulling him close.

Eda clutching Hilda's hand.

Their mother, beginning to bleed, her face, her arms, her clothing, turning slowly red.

See? Wulf said, not to her mother, but to her, to Hilda. *See what I can do, just with my mind.*

Hilda's always broke there. Skipped, like a stone over a clear mountain lake. She could look down if she wanted to, but she never wanted to.

Hilda knew what had happened.

They had all died, in front of her.

He hoped to break her. He did break her.

And after, he set her free, telling her to return when she understood her own power, when she was ready to use it.

"He's still alive," her father said over and over in her dreams.

He's still alive.

Even though they said they killed him.

Even though they said he would never hurt anyone again.

***

SHE HAD SIX DIFFERENT GUNS scattered around her kitchen. She kept the shades drawn and the windows closed, despite the god-awful heat. She didn't want anyone to look inside, see the guns, the bullets, the bits and pieces of other guns, of bombs.

Bits and pieces of her indecision.

The best way to kill a man.

There were so many.

And, in the case of Wulf, so few.

She had three fears about his farm. First, she knew if she got too close, he would sense her. Not all mages could sense magic, but the powerful mages, they could. *She* could, and she was nowhere near as powerful as he was.

As he had become.

As he had become before everyone spoke of his death.

As he should still be.

Second, she worried that someone would see her and report her, or try to stop her, or recognize her for the outsider she was (the killer she was) and do something about it.

What they would do, she didn't know.

She could defend herself.

She merely chose not to, most of the time.

And third, she worried about the method. She was a great close-range shot. She could kill looking someone in the eye, without the slightest hesitation. She could—and had.

But distance shooting, that took skill. Skill she had, yes, but had never tested in the field. Most of her targets had allowed her to get close or had become victims of her magic.

They were of a piece—her shooting and her magic. Maybe Wulf had known that when he spared her.

Maybe he had changed her into that.

Her mind shied away from that thought, then returned like a tongue worrying a loose tooth. Was magic that corruptible? Or had he had a special skill that allowed him to corrupt?

Or had this been her magic all along?

She had never known—and the war that Wulf had started with his power grab, the war that he had championed, had led to the destruction of all the old-timers. People like her father (scholars like her father) who had kept the history of magic, half in books and half in their minds, passed down like precious heirlooms from scholar to scholar, mage to mage.

She tried not to think of that, tried not to think of how much had died with him, with all of them, in those early assaults by Wulf and his minions.

He had only killed a select few himself. The rest, he let his henchmen dispatch, and they had done so swiftly and with great aplomb. He was a great strategical thinker, a powerful man albeit slightly crazed, a man who wanted the entire world—the entire magical world—and nearly got it.

The nonmagical world would see nothing like him for nearly a hundred years. And even then, Adolf Hitler lacked the magic, lacked the wisdom, and had just a bit more crazy. Circumstances had created him.

She didn't know if circumstances had created Wulf. That knowledge died with the scholars.

With her father.

With generation after generation. Only a handful survived. Some were the least magical, so no one felt threatened by them. No one sensed them. No one searched for them.

Some hadn't come into their powers yet. (*Like Gunther*, her mind told her, and then she physically shied away. She could not think of her baby brother. Thinking of him destroyed her before. It might—it would?—it could destroy her again.)

And some, an even smaller handful, used their powers to escape.

She liked to think she was part of that handful. She had escaped. But her escape wasn't heroic, like the escapes of so many others she later met.

Her escape had come because Wulf had let her free.

Had he foreseen what she would become?

Had her mother?

That simple closing of the eyes, perhaps it hadn't been a signal. Perhaps it had been fear, dislike, disgust. Perhaps she had seen what her daughter could be.

An assassin.

An assassin for hire.

An assassin for hire who usually relished her work.

She put her face in her hands.

God. What had she become?

***

SHE FOUND HIM on the tree-lined street where they had grown up. Jacob Weidman, her childhood best friend. Only the street was no longer tree-lined. It wasn't even fair to call it a street any longer.

She had come back to Berlin twice before. The first time, after the Franco-Prussian war, to see if anything had changed.

It hadn't. Not to the naked eye anyway. Inside, she could sense the difference: there was no more magic here.

It had made her uncomfortable to stand near her old house, and not just because of the memories. But also because something had been there, a sense memory, an impression, a bit of darkness or the ghostly remains of a long, horrible, lingering death.

She had left Berlin then, left Germany, returning only after the Great War, once again brought to her childhood home by a compulsion she wasn't sure she understood.

The house remained. Some of the trees were gone, re-placed by younger, healthier trees. One of the nearby hous-es had expanded. Another had disappeared completely.

But that sense of anguish was long gone, replaced by something else, a defeat, maybe, among the people who still lived here.

People without magic. People who suffered for choosing the wrong leaders and following them blindly.

This time, she couldn't stay. She need the basics like everyone else, and she saw no point in living in a place without adequate food, without a solid currency.

Without hope.

So she left again.

Only to return after the Second War, compelled by a dream, by her father's voice.

He's still alive.

She wasn't sure why that had brought her here—to the neighborhood that was no longer a neighborhood. No trees, no houses. The Allies had left rubble.

The area still stank of rot, and she knew—a year after the war ended—that the stench didn't come from old corpses, but from new ones. People who had buried themselves in the rubble, or had simply died here, trying to find somewhere else to survive.

No one dug them up, no one searched for them. Berlin was a defeated, divided city, cold and terrified. The Germans all disavowed their recent past (*I was in the resistance*, they would say. *Or I never believed in him anyway. I kept my head down. I did not want to be noticed*). Everyone knew they lied, and no one really cared.

For some reason known only to yet another set of leaders, the Allies had divided Berlin down the middle. The Soviet East and the European West. Both parts, gray and hopeless, but those in the Soviet East, even more hopeless, even more frightened, not sure if they had traded one crazy man for another.

Fortunately, or perhaps unfortunately, her old home was in the European West. She had gone there, her stomach queasy—not just from the smell—her teeth clenched, terrified of what she would find.

And it was worse, worse than she expected.

Because in her mind, that house had always remained, a tribute to her father, to a life—for all five of the dead—that should have continued, in comfort and style and warmth and love.

She sank to her knees on the rubble near where the home had been—she wasn't even sure if she was close—and heard:

"He's still alive, you know."

The same voice she had heard in her dreams. The voice she had followed here.

A voice, she now realized, too nasal to be her father's. His had been rich, deep, musical. He always sounded like he was singing, even when he was not.

This voice had no music at all.

The voice had invaded her dreams.

Her mind.

She looked up, saw Jacob Weidman sitting on a stoop, just as she had first seen him when they were all of three years old. One of her first memories, one of her firmest.

Little Jacob Weidman. Thin, blond, pale, and beautiful in a small-boy way.

Maybe if the house still stood, if the world had gone in a different direction, they would live on this street, in her family's home or in his family's, raising their own children, grandchildren, and the various greats, keeping the books and passing the stories that she had learned from her own father. The history, the secrets, the lore.

And they would joke, she and Jacob, about that meeting on the stoop, all those years ago (nearly a century ago), and they would laugh about destiny and love and the Way Things Work Out.

But he was not a little boy any longer, and she was not a dreamy-eyed little girl.

He was lanky, his blond hair now a muddy brown. His face, once chubby and red-cheeked, the epitome of German childhood joy, now taut, too thin for lines, but carrying suggestions of them all the same. Frown lines, anger lines, lines suggesting a hatred barely suppressed.

He stood when he saw her, brushing off the dust off the back of his pants. That movement remained the same: He had done that the day he met her, only with more energy and verve—a little boy, who would get trouble if his parents saw how dirty he had become.

"He's still alive," Jacob said for the third time.

And because she was angry, because she hated the violation, because she had come here and seen the destruction that had been inevitable, but hurt all the same, she said, "Why should I care?"

Jacob flinched. Just a small flinch. Enough to let her know that her harshness had hit its mark.

"He killed our families," Jacob said.

"And since then, millions of families have died," she said. "The history of humanity. Genocide on a mass scale."

He didn't flinch this time. Instead, he threaded his hands before him. She could sense him, willing himself to be calm.

"They told me you had changed. I hadn't believed it."

So flat, so unemotional, as if he didn't care that the bright, joyful little girl who used to laugh with him, who would probably have become his wife in another life, had become this thing, this creature who lashed out, any way she could.

"Who are 'they?'" she asked.

But she had a hunch. An old man she'd met on a train to Vienna before the Great War, just a bit of magic hanging off him, like an untrimmed thread. A woman her age, who had served her tea in Babington's near the Spanish Steps one hot summer in Rome.

And others. She had met so many—that's how she knew the magical still survived—but she had never joined them.

She never wanted to, no matter how much they begged. No matter how much they claimed she was needed.

"We're building our numbers again," Jacob said. "We can have a community once more."

"But?" she asked.

"We have to get rid of the last of the evil." He seemed so serious. "We don't want them to wipe us out."

The word "again" was implied. Even though the last of the elders used their dying powers to get rid of Wulf and his minions, somehow the plan failed. Wulf lived.

If she could believe Jacob.

Wulf's empire was gone, but Wulf remained, undefeatable. Waiting, lurking, going in for the kill.

Although that didn't make sense. The longer he waited, the more his enemies would build their strength. His minions had destroyed the powerful. They had destroyed the elders and their memories, the scholarship, the research, the spells that enhanced the white magic.

But scholarship could be reconstructed. Research rebuilt. Magic rediscovered. And as new generations were born, the powerful returned. For only so much of it was hereditary. Sometimes great mages appeared with no familial antecedents.

Gunther would have been such a mage.

Had he lived.

But she didn't challenge Jacob. She still had enough respect for him—for their shared past—that she couldn't speak to him with as much disrespect as she would have used with someone else.

Instead, she said—her tone emphasizing her doubt—"You have proof?"

"Yes," he said. "We have a lot of proof."

***

IN THE END, she decided on the rifle, and two pistols, stuck in her belt as if she were a *caballero*.

Because it didn't matter if she lived.

What mattered was that he died.

She waited two days, hoping that the weather would break. When it did not, she drove back to the farm, wearing her dusty clothing. She had cut off her hair. She no longer cared how she looked (she had a hunch she would not survive this anyway. She would never get another chance to dress like a woman, so why should her vanity get in the way of her mission?) She brought beef jerky, six old Coke bottles filled with water, and more ammunition than she probably needed. She also brought the binoculars, although the rifle's scope would probably have done as well.

She left Buenos Aires two hours before dawn, one of the few vehicles on the road, and bounced her way over potholes on the dusty roads that led into the valley.

It was already hot. It was going to get hotter. She tried not to think about that.

She parked the truck two miles away from the farm, just as the road twisted into the valley. She had found a small area with trees, enough to shelter the truck from casual glances.

She spent fifteen minutes pouring as much dirt over the truck as she could. Then she gathered everything into a pack and hiked the two miles. She wore the truck's keys around her neck, but wasn't sure she would need them.

She wasn't sure she would need anything again.

***

THE PROOF JACOB SHOWED HER made her eyes hurt.

He took her to an office in a rebuilt section of the city, not too far from the Soviet East. The office, up five flights, was little more than a closet. A desk dominated the room. A boarded up window let in little light, and a single bulb swayed overhead.

She thought, at first, of all those clichéd interrogation scenes from American movies—the overhead bulb swaying, the light driving the criminal to confess—then Jacob turned on a desk lamp, dispelling that illusion.

He pulled over a chair, one that did not match the chair behind the desk.

Nothing matched, and it took her a moment to realize it was all salvage—surviving bits and pieces taken from destroyed buildings, ruined houses, flattened neighborhoods.

She sat at the edge of the chair, suddenly unwilling to touch much of anything in the room.

Then she asked again for proof.

She expected a few papers, but mostly, she thought she would see images. A few photographs, and then a magical presentation, like one she had seen on the only other magical job she had ever done right after the Great War.

The mage had opened a tunnel in the air, and through it, she could see the target as he was at that moment, preparing himself a solitary supper.

That target was the only one she remembered in action. She remembered him as a scrawny man, making himself dinner, not as a corpse she had kicked into an open grave.

But Jacob's magic did not go to the visual. That was why he had projected his own voice into her mind.

No, he gave her nothing magical at all.

Instead, he thrust ledgers at her. Ledgers from banks, from private accounts, from brokerages all over the world, some (according to the notations) painstakingly copied from the originals. Later ledgers were telexes or photostats or both.

Jacob started to explain these to her, but she shushed him.

She might be doing a job that required little intellectual finesse, but that didn't mean she failed to understand balance sheets. Once she found the beginning of it, she realized whose financial ledgers she was looking at.

The Great Wulf's.

The ledgers from before he "died" told a story all their own. Money moved from one country to another, from one account to another. New names formed. New accounts established. Some only numbered, some by name, some in Germany, most elsewhere.

Each account then followed as if it were a separate person. Money tracked, wealth compounded, more identities branching off like bits of trees.

"You found him through his money?" she asked, looking up, her eyes aching.

Jacob nodded, a half smile on his thin lips. Proud of all the work.

All the mundane, non-magical work.

She put her hands over her eyes. She couldn't tell if they ached from the tiny print, the careful scrawls she had stared at for hours now, or because her power was starting to flare, or because it all seemed so simple, an easy, overlooked way of tracking a man she had thought—they all had thought—too powerful to be found.

For the next two days, she studied the ledgers. She wanted to see if there were any flaws. She didn't want to act if there was any chance at a mistake.

There was not.

Some of the money vanished in the 1870s—the Franco-Prussian war, the American Depression. More vanished in the early 1900s as another worldwide collapse threatened, but stopped this time by intervention of an American named Morgan, whom some thought to be a wizard himself. And even more disappeared in 1929.

But Wulf had built up so much money, in so many names, in so many accounts, in so many countries, that the funds overwhelmed the losses. He never lost it all, and he always gained a great deal in the good times.

He was fantastically wealthy.

But he was in exile.

And worse, in 1947, he was a German in exile.

Which to the rest of the world—the nonmagical world—meant only one thing.

A German in exile meant a Nazi in exile, running from his criminal past.

Wulf was running from his criminal past, so that much was true.

He was German as well.

And he had committed mass murder.

Only of a kind the non-magical world would never prosecute.

So it was up to her.

***

SHE COULD HAVE BUILT a shield around herself, so that the sun wouldn't bake her and she wouldn't feel the heat, but she didn't. She was afraid to use any magic this close to Wulf. She was afraid he would sense it.

But as she lay in the dirt, the sun frying her fair skin, she wondered if he hadn't sensed her already.

She hadn't seen him since the first few days of her surveillance, yet she knew he hadn't moved. His money hadn't moved—she checked with Jacob—and neither had the big green Chevrolet Wulf used to get to Buenos Aires.

If he were going to leave, he would have taken the car. He didn't want to use his magic. He didn't dare—he could be tracked through it.

He was here.

She knew it.

She just had to wait for him to appear.

She had the rifle braced on a little tripod she had purchased at a photography shop. She had learned long ago that little tripods like that held the rifle, keeping it secure in a way that her hands, in position for hours, could not.

Her Coke bottles were buried in the dirt so that they didn't reflect the light (and she liked to think that they stayed cooler, although cooler was, at this moment, a relative term).

She had eaten some jerky already, not because she was hungry, but because she had learned long ago that jerky had salt, and a person in the sun needed salt.

Even after several hours, she felt fresh, ready.

Although a part of her, a small part, wanted this to end. She didn't want to think about Wulf any more. To think about (Gunther) the lovely lost house on the beautiful vanished tree-lined street and the life that could have been.

So she forced her mind away from her family, from her revenge, made herself focus on the task.

Which held her for another hour at least, until her dry lips made her realize that she needed to drink or she would be useless.

She sipped from a nearby bottle and continued watching the house. The dusty windows showed no signs of life. The yard looked the same as it had days before.

All she had was a strange confidence that he hadn't left.

She had learned to trust those confidences. She believed (although she did not know) that those feelings were a part of her magic.

She really didn't know what, exactly, her magic was supposed to be. Magic divided itself into parts, distributing itself reluctantly. One person got a bit of this, another got a bit of that.

Through practice and concentration, the bit of this might become a lot of this, but never did it become a bit of that.

She didn't practice much. She had a few skills—she could build shields, and she could augment harm if she really tried.

But she didn't know much else.

She didn't want to think about it.

Magic brought too much of what could have been.

So she waited, and made herself remember the other times.

The times she hadn't used magic at all. The times she got paid, and the times she hadn't.

The times she found a satisfaction in the death itself.

***

SHE FOUND THE FAT MAN in the forest outside of Berlin after her first meeting with Jacob. She had actually contracted the job, going to a friend of hers in the Haganah and asking for an assignment.

The Haganah, the underground Jewish defense force based in Palestine, actually had squads of its own that pursued ex-Nazis and members of the Gestapo, but they also had some high-value targets that they couldn't seem to catch or kill on their own.

She had known that for months because her friends in the Haganah had asked her before, and she had said (wrongly, she later realized) that it was not her fight.

She made it her fight after seeing the ledgers. She needed to do something, to get rid of the restlessness, to prove herself to herself.

So they told her about the fat man. He was a high-ranking member of the Gestapo posing as a regular citizen. In his arrogance, he stayed in Berlin, thinking he could pass as a beleaguered German, when in fact, he had murdered dozens, maybe hundreds all on his own.

He confessed to them all before she killed him. He confessed, not because she threatened him, but because she was blond and blue eyed, with round German cheeks.

Fraulein, he said, *we are the same, you and I. Inside your heart, you know that these people do not belong on the Earth. You know I did nothing wrong.*

She didn't answer him.

Instead, she shot him in the face, just so that he would shut up.

She should have kept him alive long enough to take names, dates, all the things that the Haganah wanted. Or at least a location of files, so that names and dates could be confirmed.

But the bastard had commiserated with her, as if she had understood him. As if she knew what kind of man he truly was.

We are the same, you and I.

But they were not the same.

They were not.

She would have told him that, if she hadn't already shut him up.

***

HER SCALP PRICKLED in the heat. To keep her mind off the sweat gathering under her shirt, she went through all her killings from the fat bastard all the way back to the dapper little man in Victorian London who had taken it upon himself to slaughter all the prostitutes in Whitechapel.

She didn't remember the people she had killed for money.

Only the ones she had killed for the right reasons.

Like she would kill Wulf.

Suddenly, there he was. In front of her scope, too close to shoot.

He just appeared. She raised her head, but he was already gone.

She felt a shiver run down her back.

An illusion? The real Wulf? She couldn't tell. She wasn't sure.

Then he was beside her. Thin, older, the man she had seen days before.

He smiled. He was missing one of his front teeth.

"I knew you would be come back to me," he said in German, and vanished again.

Leaving footprints in the dirt.

The real Wulf. Did he lack the power to create an illusion? Or had he realized that the use of magic would bring everyone to him, so he might as well go all out?

He probably thought he was fooling her. He probably thought she believed him an illusion.

But he wasn't.

He appeared to her front, then on her right.

Front, side.

She felt him the third time, behind her, creating his own breeze. She didn't turn around, trusting (perhaps foolishly) that he wouldn't hurt her.

He wanted her.

She had a sense—oddly—that he needed her power.

"You knew I was here," she said, still facing forward.

"You're hard to miss, my dear," he said. "You send a wave of magic ahead of you."

She hadn't heard that before, but it did not surprise her.

"Such hatred in you," he said, with pleasure. "It gives you power."

And then he was gone. Another breeze told her that. Gone as if he had never been.

She moved her hands away from the rifle's butt, slowly, carefully. Her muscles were not sore. She had learned how to keep them fresh. She had done this too many times before.

She slid her knees under her torso, crouching, ready.

He appeared again.

In front of her.

She had expected him at the side.

"You cannot predict everything," he said, and laughed.

The laugh was cold. She remembered it as vividly as she remembered (Eda, screaming) her family, her father's eyes, her mother's sad smile.

He vanished again, but not before she saw him, truly saw him.

Tall, thin, old. She had noted the old before. It diminished him, accented the gray pallor of his skin, made him seem more unwell than he had seemed in that dungeon, all those years ago.

Perhaps she was going to do him a favor when she killed him.

Then she realized that thought was one he sent her. It did not belong to her. He was trying to convince her that killing him was what he wanted, knowing that if she believed that, she wouldn't do it.

He was playing with her mind.

Somehow she had let her mind become porous.

First Jacob had invaded.

Now Wulf.

No one would do so again.

She whirled to the left.

Wulf appeared just as she did that, just as she pulled out her pistol.

Before he could speak, she shot him.

The power of the shot sent him tumbling backwards, leaving a brain-and-blood trail in the dust.

She stood, half dizzy, her legs weaker than she expected, worried suddenly that she hadn't shot Wulf, that she had shot someone he had used as a foil.

So she clambered toward the body, her legs aching, her clothes clinging to her overheated skin.

It was him. His features, so familiar from her dreams, had relaxed in death. The shot was clean. A perfect, solid little hole in his forehead, the center of his power.

He was dead.

No one—magical or not—survived a shot like that.

She sank onto the earth, feeling a relief so profound that she nearly passed out. Her father would have approved. (Except that he believed in comfort, not vengeance.) Her mother would have been proud. (Had Hilda done this when the family was still alive). Jacob would be as relieved as she was.

Indeed, came the thought, and she wasn't sure if it was her own. At the moment, she didn't care.

She blinked, then looked at Wulf's corpse. Truly looked at it, as it was now.

He had been a small man. A small *old* man with tattered clothes and bad teeth.

All those years, she had thought him the embodiment of evil.

Jacob had thought him the embodiment of evil.

Had they given him too much credit?

Or had their belief given him the power to survive?

She would never know. Because she did not want to know.

She did not want to examine him or her role in his survival.

Her role in his life.

She picked up her rifle, packed her supplies in her bag, wiped the impression of her body out of the dirt.

Then she stood over him one last time.

She had buried all the others, the ones she had killed. She had put them into the ground, disposing of them in the most humane way she knew.

But she would give him no courtesy. Let the jackals get him. Let the sun bleach him to bone.

So much hatred in you. It gives you power.

"Yes," she said as she walked away. "Yes. It does."

About the Author

USA Today bestselling author Kristine Kathryn Rusch writes in almost every genre. Generally, she uses her real name (Rusch) for most of her writing. Under that name, she publishes bestselling science fiction and fantasy, award-winning mysteries, acclaimed mainstream fiction, controversial nonfiction, and the occasional romance. Her novels have made bestseller lists around the world and her short fiction has appeared in eighteen best of the year collections. She has won more than twenty-five awards for her fiction, including the Hugo, *Le Prix Imaginales,* the *Asimov's* Readers Choice award, and the *Ellery Queen Mystery Magazine* Readers Choice Award.

To keep up with everything she does, go to kristine kathrynrusch.com and sign up for her newsletter. To track her many pen names and series, see their individual websites (krisnelscott.com, kristinegrayson.com, krisdelake. com, retrievalartist.com, divingintothewreck.com). She lives and occasionally sleeps in Oregon.

Be the first to know!

Just sign up for the Kristine Kathryn Rusch newsletter, and keep up with the latest news, releases and so much more—even the occasional giveaway.

To sign up, go to kristinekathrynrusch.com.

But wait! There's more. Sign up for the WMG Publishing newsletter, too, and get the latest news and releases from all of the WMG authors and lines, including Kristine Grayson, Kris Nelscott, Dean Wesley Smith, *Fiction River: An Original Anthology Magazine, Smith's Monthly,* and so much more.

Just go to wmgpublishing.com and click on Newsletter.

Read more in the Faerie Justice series with *Show Trial*,
available from your favorite bookseller.